In a state of pani
knob, twisted it, an
"Funny Bone" Fenimore was right behind him, the knife in his hand. But when the blade came down, it narrowly missed the fleeing fullback, stabbing the rail of the stairwell instead.

Bone extracted the blade and took a couple of steps. Puffing from his exertions, he staggered to a stop. The world seemed to rotate under his feet, and he wavered. Glancing up, he saw the big kid blubbering incoherently as he scrambled out of sight.

Sitting down heavily on the steps, Bone looked at the knife in his hand. What was he doing with it? He didn't remember having a knife when he came into the club. He looked back at the door to the room and was surprised to see none of the partyers had followed him out. Staggering to his feet, Bone walked back to the room and, for a moment, was startled. The room looked different. It was old and rotting.

He rubbed his eyes and looked again. Now, the room was bright and new. Ashley and the others were sitting at the table where he'd left them. He looked once more at the knife in his hand, but saw that he had been mistaken somehow. It was nothing but a pen. He laughed at that.

Tossing it away, he stepped back into the room to join the others.

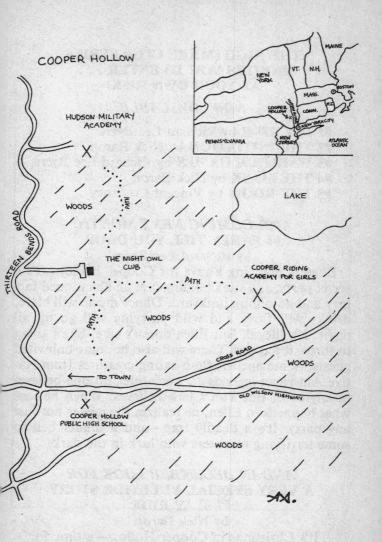

#5: THE ROOM

Vincent Courtney

Z·FAVE
KENSINGTON PUBLISHING CORP.

Z*FAVE BOOKS are published by

Kensington Publishing Corp.
475 Park Avenue South
New York, NY 10016

First Printing: October, 1993

Printed in the United States of America

One

Bone Fenimore saw his victim standing at his locker down the hall. He ducked behind a corner in the science building at Cooper High and waited. The shiny metal paper clip in his hand felt slippery from his sweaty fingertips. A girl, Mary Kelly, walked by him and stared. He blew a kiss at her and she rolled her eyes and continued down the hall. Bone focused his attention back to Alvin Merritt, his intended victim. Alvin was the star fullback for the Cooper High football team. He was also a braggart and picked on Bone unmercifully. Now at the right moment, the skinny Fenimore would have his revenge.

Alvin closed his locker and started strutting toward the corner where Bone was waiting.

Bone smiled as his victim approached. "Come on, big shot," Bone said to himself as he got the hook ready to strike.

Alvin kept coming.

"Come on."

Alvin stopped for a moment and looked to his left. Bone tensed. Had he been seen?

The big fullback reached into his back pocket and

pulled out his comb. He combed his hair while he looked at his reflection in the window of Mrs. Horst's room.

Bone sighed.

Alvin put the comb back into his pocket and started down the hall again.

"What's up, Truck?" he said when he saw his buddy, Mark Calhoun, a tackle on the team, sitting on a bench about fifty feet away.

"You, Bull," a smiling Mark said pointing at his friend.

Alvin waved and walked past the spot where Bone Fenimore was waiting.

Bone readied the hook. He took a quick breath and made his move

It was over in a second.

"Hey, watch it, dweeb," Alvin said as Bone bumped into him and the hook found its mark.

"Sorry," Bone said in his best apologetic voice.

"Next time, I'll knock you on your scrawny ass."

"Right," Bone said, stifling a grin as he watched the big man on campus walk away with a two foot yellow tail, with purple polka dots, hanging from his belt loop.

Jennifer Struthers giggled as Merritt strutted by her. Her friends, Eva Van Hudmon and Susan Buren, joined her. Across the hall, Tony Sims, Bone's best friend, smiled and shook his head as he looked at the colorful tail streaming behind the star fullback and then over at his friend. Bone gave him a thumbs-up signal.

Tony couldn't believe the lengths that Bone sometimes went to, just to get a laugh. Antagonizing Alvin Merritt wasn't the brightest thing for anyone to do. And for someone like Bone, who weighed in at a hundred and thirty pounds and couldn't fight his way out of a wet paper lunch sack, it bordered on insanity. But Tony had to admit that it was pretty hilarious to see the cocky football stud strutting down the hall, trailing a yellow tail with purple polka dots. And the laughing students Merritt left in his wake apparently agreed.

Bone ran over to where Tony was standing.

"Look at the rare speciman of a Bull with a polka dot tail. Pretty impressive, eh?"

"It'll be impressive when Alvin makes you eat that thing."

"I took care of that possibility by making the tail out of rice paper," Bone said smiling. "If rice's good for the Chinese, it's good for me."

Tony fought back a grin. "What about the paper clip?"

"No prob. Full of iron."

Tony laughed. "You finish your Spanish homework?"

"*Si, si, señor.* Mucho finisho."

"Let me see it for a sec."

"Oh, no *señor,* tha' would be cheating," Bone said. "We don' do that."

"I just want to see the verb tenses."

"Okay, but it will cost you some pesos."

"Just give it to me, Fenimore."

Bone reached into his folder and pulled out his Spanish homework. He handed it to his friend.

9

As Tony checked his answers against his friend's, Bone asked him, "So are we going to the Night Owl Club tonight?"

"Are you sure this is right?" Tony said, pointing at one of the answers.

"Yeah, I'm sure. So are we going?"

"If my aunt is feeling okay, but I don't know." Tony looked at the answer again. "You sure about number three? It doesn't look right."

"Man, who has the A in Spanish and who's barely pulling a C?"

"Chill out, so it's right," Tony said.

"I hope Cindy's gonna be there tonight," Bone said. Cindy Macleod was the pretty blond girl who sat in front of him in math class and Pam Williams' best friend. Pam was Tony's steady squeeze.

Tony looked up from the homework paper. "Why? Every time she's hanging with us, you don't ask her to dance or make a move on her."

"She likes Kevin."

"Just because they were dancing at the masquerade together last week doesn't mean they like each other."

"How do you know?"

"Pam told me, you dork. How else would I know?"

Bone shrugged as the warning bell rang for third period.

"Well, I better get my butt in gear. I have to go all the way to the gym," Tony said as he handed Bone his Spanish homework and headed down the hallway.

"See you at lunch," Bone said.

Tony walked backward as he said, "I'm going home at noon. I have to drive my aunt to the doctor. It's

10

Friday checkup time."

"Oh, okay, so call me this afternoon about hitting it tonight."

"Yeah," Tony shouted as he turned around and hustled toward the gymnasium.

Bone started to head for his English class when he discovered that he had left his English book in his locker. "Damn," he said under his breath as he ran to the locker to get his book.

As Bone approached the locker, he saw something hanging from his lock and a sick lumpy worm of fear dropped into his gut. He slowed down when he saw the yellow and purple polka dotted tail with the words "Dead Meat," scrawled across it.

Bone heard footsteps running toward him. Quickly, he looked around for an ambush, but it was too late. Alvin Merritt was charging.

Bone screamed.

Bull smiled, lowered his shoulder, and prepared to collide with the skinny clown.

The big teen was nearly upon him when Bone fell to the ground and tripped the big fullback. Caught off-guard, Merritt slammed into the unyielding metal of the lockers and Bone took off running toward the English building.

Alvin staggered for a moment. But the collision was no worse than the time he'd had his bell rung by Jake Simson, the star linebacker at Hudson Military Academy. He quickly recovered and gave chase, but it was too late. Bone had a lead that couldn't be covered. The skinny teenager was not much in a fight, but he could run like a rabbit especially if he was scared.

The last bell rang as Bone made it to the door of his English class. Before he opened the door to go inside, he turned around and saw Bull standing at the end of the hallway. The big teen pointed at Fenimore, then slammed his fist into a nearby locker. The clanging sent a chill up Bone's spine.

He stepped into the room.

"You're late, Harold," Mr. Kitchens stated as he lowered the glasses on his nose and peered over them. "See me after class for your detention slip."

"But Mr. Kitchens, I have a reason for being late."

Kitchens folded his arms. "And what, pray tell, is that?"

Fenimore hesitated and then began his story. "Well, while I was walking to class there was this bright white light and it came down and these skinny little pale dudes with black eyes came out and zapped me with this ray . . ."

The class cracked up. Kitchens raised his hand to silence them.

"Go ahead."

"So these skinny pale dudes zapped me with a ray, and I was frozen."

There was more laughter from the class as Bone continued, "Then they started to examine me, but the bell rang, and I guess it disrupted their freeze ray. So I got away, but the close encounter made me late."

Kitchens took off his glasses. "I see. Well, now that you've explained it all to me, I think your little pale friends with the black eyes should have to serve detention with you since they were responsible for making you late. Now please sit down and be quiet, Mr. Fenimore."

The class laughed as Bone nodded and went to sit down. When the rush from the laughter died, Bone began to consider the fullback's punched locker warning.

Why'd I have to hang the tail on the big jerk? Why did I have to do it? Bone smiled. Because it was funny that's why. And funny is what I am. Harold "Funny Bone" Fenimore. Bone for short. Class clown soon to be punching bag. Oh well, every comic has to suffer before he makes it to the big time.

His mind wandered to Cindy Macleod and the Night Owl Club. Maybe tonight would be the night he would gather up the courage to ask her to dance. Yeah, they would fast dance a few songs and then the music would change to a romantic ballad. He would ask her to stay on the floor with him. She would say yes, and it would be wonderful as they danced cheek to cheek. And then . . . maybe she would kiss him and they would fall in love . . .

Yeah and Bull Merritt's gonna forget all about your little joke with the tail, reality whispered in his ear.

Bone shook his head to erase the thought of Merritt's vengeance and turned his attention to Mr. Kitchens who was talking about Herman Melville and the great white whale known as Moby Dick. Fenimore started to say that he knew a man one time who had that disease, but thought better of it. He already had one day's detention and that particular joke would surely get him a week's worth.

* * *

The day passed quickly. Bone Fenimore found himself walking out of the classroom and immediately looking for Alvin Merritt. Seeing that the coast was clear, Bone took a few steps. A hand reached out and grabbed him. He gasped and shielded himself from the punches he knew were coming.

"What's wrong, Bone?" a girl's voice said. It was Cindy Macleod.

"Oh, uh, hey, Cindy, uh, nothing," Bone said, trying to smile nonchalantly and straighten up to his normal posture. "I was, uh, just imagining Mrs. Ross giving me a Japanese massage with her curly arthritic toes, and it scared me."

Cindy laughed. "That's so gross."

Bone nodded. "It's a terrible recurring daydream."

Cindy shook her head. "Where do you come up with that stuff, Bone?"

"I dunno. I guess it just oozes from my sick little head."

Cindy smiled and changed the subject. "I wanted to ask you something."

"Oh, really," Bone said. Maybe she wanted to see if they were going to the Night Owl Club. Maybe she wanted him to take . . .

"Did you get the last homework problem that Mrs. Ross gave us? I was talking to Mary."

Bone tried to maintain his smile. "Oh, uh, yeah, sure." He reached into his folder and found his notes. He handed them to her.

"Thanks." She looked through the notes and found the question. She wrote it into her notebook and gave the notes back to Bone. "I'll see you," Cindy said as she started walking away.

Suddenly, Bone was seized by a momentary burst of courage. He was going to ask her to go out with him. He raised his finger, "Oh, Cindy, uh, wait."

Cindy stopped. She turned to face Fenimore and he looked straight into her pretty blue eyes. He smiled, lost in her gaze.

"What is it? I have to catch the bus," Cindy said.

Bone snapped out of his daze. "Oh, uh, you, uh, you want to, uh, you didn't get the other problem."

"Which one?"

Bone reached into his folder and pulled out the first sheet of paper he felt. He looked at it. "Oh, I'm sorry, that was from yesterday. Sorry."

Cindy shrugged. "It's cool. Now I gotta catch the bus."

"Oh, yeah, okay."

"See ya."

Watching Cindy walk away, Bone wished that he had asked her to go out with him. He cursed himself for his lack of guts.

As he started for the bike racks in the parking lot, he reconsidered his actions. Maybe it was for the best. Chances are she would've laughed at him and turned him down. Better to play it safe and avoid the humiliation.

Then, Bone thought he saw Bull Merritt in his letterman jacket up ahead of him. He turned and went around the building to avoid a possible confrontation.

When he got to the parking lot, he found his bike

and unlocked the chain. Climbing aboard, he started to pedal for home. He didn't hear the blue Mustang start its engine, pull out of its parking space, and start to follow him.

Tony Sims lifted his Aunt Ann, into the van. She smiled weakly. The doctor had told them that there was no change in her condition. Tony had lost his mother and father over eight years ago in a terrible car accident. Aunt Ann had become his legal guardian then, and he had been happy with her. Why did he have to lose her, too?

The lung cancer was slowly eating her away. Tony had warned his aunt to stop smoking, but she hadn't. Whenever he'd complained to her about it, she'd always told him that it was her body and she could do what she wanted. He guessed she thought, like most smokers do, that cancer only happened to other people. And now they were both paying the price for her actions. She with her life, he with his broken heart.

"Tony, I don't understand it. I should be getting better," Aunt Ann said, then coughed as her nephew helped her into the seat.

Tony nodded while his heart broke. The doctors had told them that there was little hope of survival for his aunt and yet she still clung to the belief that she would get better.

She coughed with a phlegmy rattle. "Maybe next time."

"Yeah, next time," Tony said.

Tony buckled her seat belt and went around to the driver's side of the car. He climbed in and started the van.

As they drove home, Tony glanced over at his aunt. In one year's time, she had gone from a vibrant out-going woman to a withered shell waiting to be emptied of life. Her hair was patchy from the chemotherapy. Her skin was pale and wrinkled. She looked a thousand years old.

"Why so sad, Tony? I told you I'm going to get better," she said.

"Aunt Ann, I want that more than anything, believe me, but the doctors said . . ."

"Doctors! What do they know? There are things much stronger than their puny medicines and treatments."

Tony knew that his aunt was referring to her faith in God. She was a religious woman who attended church at least three times a week, but she was cool about it. She never preached or forced Tony to go with her. In fact, she rarely, if ever, talked about her beliefs. She told Tony that he was old enough to make his own decisions about religion and let it go at that. Her acknowledgment of his independence was one of the things he loved most about his aunt. God, how he was going to miss her. Tony felt the tears well up in his eyes.

"Please, don't do that." she said as the tears formed in her eyes. "Listen, I know I'm going to get better. I swear it. Any day this thing inside me is going to go into remission and I will get better." The words sounded hollow coming from the cracked lips of one

17

so close to death.

Tony looked away from his aunt and wiped his eyes with the sleeve of his shirt. "Yeah," he said with little conviction.

Seeing her nephew's depression, Tony's aunt changed the subject. "So how's Bone doing? He hasn't come around lately."

"Oh, he's doing good." Tony said grateful that his aunt had changed the subject. She was so much stronger than he was.

"Does he have a girlfriend yet?"

"Are you kidding?" Tony said grinning. "Bone's too busy playing his jokes. But I think that's because he's so afraid of getting rejected."

Aunt Ann nodded.

"I mean he's a funny guy and the kids at school like to watch him crack on people and stuff, but when everybody starts, like, pairing up at a dance or at the club he just kinda gets lost. He has trouble fitting in."

Tony's aunt smiled. "Well, maybe he just hasn't found the right girl."

"Maybe. I just hope that she's a girl who likes to run."

"What makes you say that?"

"Well, today Bone played a joke on one of the meanest dudes in school," Tony said, then began to explain the joke Bone had played on Alvin Merritt.

While Tony told the "Tale of the Tail," the subject of that story was riding his bike straight into the jaws of retribution.

* * *

As Bone started down the street leading to his house, he heard the engine of a car rev behind him. He turned and looked straight into the eyes of Bull Merritt. Sitting beside the fullback in the car was Truck Calhoun.

Judging from the look on Bull's face, Bone expected Merritt to hit him with the car, but the jock just drove past him. Bone was relieved until he saw Truck hurling a broom that caught in the spokes of his bike. The front wheel stopped spinning immediately and Bone was airborne over the handlebars. He landed in a heap.

The car pulled over and Merritt grabbed Bone before he had a chance to get up. Three quick slaps later, Bone's eyes were watery and his cheeks felt like he had a mouthful of wasps.

"Think you're a funnyman, huh, Harold," Merritt sneered as he slapped Bone again. "Hanging your little tail on me."

"C'mon, man, it was just a joke," Bone pleaded.

Merritt slapped him again. "I don't like being part of a joke, dipwad."

Tears streamed down Bone's face as he struggled to break free from the powerful grasp of the football player.

"Hey, Truck, gimme that spray can in the car," Merritt yelled to his friend in the Mustang.

"Come on, Bull, I won't mess with you anymore," Bone said, trying to get away from Merritt.

"Damned straight you won't, dipwad."

Through blurry eyes, Bone saw Truck go to the Mustang and pull out a can of paint. The cap on the

19

can was purple.

"Now we're gonna see who looks good in polka dots," Alvin said, laughing.

Bone struggled to break out of the fullback's grip, but he was no match for Bull.

"Spray him good," Truck said. "I want to see what a purple polka-dotted geek looks like."

"Yeah," Merritt said, "so do I." He shoved Bone toward the big lineman. "Hold this dipwad so I can paint him. Maybe he can tell us how it tastes, too."

Bone stumbled and then kicked Truck in the shin as hard as he could. The big kid shouted in surprise as he dropped the paint can and reached for his wounded leg.

"You little dork," Alvin said as he reached for the can of paint. Bone grabbed it first and sprayed Merritt right in the face. The jock screamed and put his hands to his face.

Bone threw the can as far as he could and took off running down the street. Truck hobbled after him.

"Truck, get in the car, man," Bull shouted as he ran for the car. The paint hadn't gotten in his eyes. His scream had been one of rage.

Running as fast as he could, Bone cut through a well manicured lawn and ran toward the backyard to escape his pursuers only to be confronted with a chain link fence. He didn't hesitate. He jumped the fence and landed in the backyard.

When he hit the ground, he paused to catch his breath. He heard a bark and turned to his left.

He saw a big Doberman and the big Doberman saw him. Bone let out a yelp and sprinted toward the fence on the other side of the yard. The Doberman started after him.

Bone was twenty feet from the fence.

The dog was halfway across the yard.

Bone almost tripped.

The dog was getting closer.

The teen glanced over his shoulder and saw the big shiny black dog with the big shiny white teeth. Maybe a spray paint job wouldn't have been so bad, he thought dismally.

Bone picked up speed.

So did the Dobie.

The race was on. Would Bone get to the fence before the dog got to Bone?

The fence was getting closer.

So was the dog.

The fence was within reach.

Bone jumped for it.

The dog jumped for Bone.

The race was over.

The dog won.

Bone fell to the ground and the watch dog was on him.

Bone felt no pain as the dog's mouth found his cheek. In fact, it tickled. It was then that Bone realized that the dog was licking him, not biting him.

Bone started laughing as the big dog lapped at his face. He tried to push him off, but the dog was as strong as he was fast.

"Stop, big guy," Bone giggled. "Come on."

The dog continued with the slobbering kisses. Suddenly, Bone thought he might drown.

"Come on. Stop."

The dog didn't stop.

Bone pushed him away.

"Fetch," he shouted, tossing an imaginary bone.

The dog wasn't buying, he kept licking.

"Sit!" Bone shouted.

The dog stopped licking him and did exactly what Bone said. The teenager got up and petted the dog's head.

"Good boy. Now stay." He stuck his hand in front of the dog's face and started to back away. He got to the fence and started to climb.

"Blitzkrieg," a voice shouted from the house and the Doberman started snarling. It jumped for Bone who was halfway over the fence. The surprised teen pulled with all his strength and toppled over the fence just as the dog's teeth snapped tight around the air where Bone's butt had just been.

The owner of the dog, a fat cruel-looking man, laughed and shouted, "Stay off my property, you punk."

"I'm a ghost, fatso," Bone said, as he disappeared into the hedge of the backyard where he had fallen. He was glad that the guard dog was trained to attack on command, not on sight. He brushed the dirt off, pulled out his shirt tail, and wiped the sweat and slobber off his face. He walked to the side of the house to get a better vantage point of the area.

Bone surveyed the street looking for the Mustang and its irate occupants. The road was deserted. Bone sighed with relief and then started to walk home.

"My bike!" he said. He couldn't leave it by the side

of the road. Someone would take it.

"Oh, man," he hissed with frustration. He started back across the lawn and into the backyard. He skirted the fence containing the Doberman and came out in back of a parked car. He peered out from behind the car to scope the area. He didn't see the Mustang. He did, however, see his bike laying by the side of the road and was relieved. He waited in back of the car for a couple of minutes and then crept out from his hiding place. There was still no sign of the car containing the football players. He hurried over to his bicycle and righted it. The spokes were bent so he straightened them as best he could in order to ride the bike. He got on the seat to test it.

The bike wobbled a bit, but worked. He looked around one more time for the Mustang, and then started for home.

When they got home, Tony helped his aunt onto the sofa where she stayed most of the day watching TV or reading. She turned on the TV to catch the end of "Oprah."

"Can I get you anything, Aunt Ann?" Tony asked.

"Maybe a glass of water," she replied.

Tony went into the kitchen and poured his aunt a glass of water. He carried it back into the living room.

"Here you go," he said.

"Thanks," she said.

"You want me to clean up the house a little tonight?"

Tony's aunt shook her head. "I'll tell you what I

want you to do. I want you to go out with your friends tonight and have a good time. You've been taking care of me all week, and I know that gets old."

"I don't mind."

"Well, I mind. Go have some fun. Why don't you and Bone go out to the Night Owl Club tonight? I know you like that place."

"We were talking about it."

"Well, go ahead and go. I feel pretty tired anyway. I think I'll just go to bed early."

"You sure?"

"I'm sure. Have some fun for me." She smiled and then coughed.

Tony smiled. "I'll try."

The phone rang.

Tony ran to answer it. He picked up the handset and said, "Hello."

"Yeah, is Mr. Grimaldi there?" a scratchy voice said.

"Sorry. There's no Mr. Grimaldi here. You have . . ."

The caller got mad and interrupted. "What do you mean, he's not there, I know he's there. Get him right now."

"Look . . ."

"Don't give me no lip, boy. When I want Grimaldi, he better be there."

Tony smiled when he recognized the voice. "What's up, Bone?"

"Nothing. Where's Mr. Grimaldi?"

"You didn't fake me out. I knew it was you."

"Oh, right, then why'd you say, there's no Mr. Grimaldi here?"

"To keep you going."

"Right."

"So what's going down?"

"Me, six feet down."

"Wait, let me guess. Bull Merritt caught up with you after school."

"Man, you must be psychic. Have you got one of those hot lines, like on TV?"

Tony laughed. "What happened?"

Bone explained what had happened with the guys and the dog.

"So what do you think? Am I still on the hit list?" Bone asked his friend.

"I dunno. Probably."

"That's what I figured," Bone replied glumly.

"Hey, you mess with fire . . ."

Bone finished Tony's sentence for him. "You get burned. Yeah, I know."

Bone changed the subject, "So how's your aunt doing?"

"She's about the same."

"Bummin'," Bone replied. "They can't do anything for her?"

"They give her pain killers and stuff, but . . . You can't stop that stuff once it spreads. Tomorrow starts the home health nurses. They'll be two shifts, and I'll help in-between. She's going to die soon, Bone. That's why the doctor arranged for the nurses."

Bone couldn't think of anything to say.

"I warned her to quit smoking those damn things and she wouldn't. Too stubborn." Tony felt a tear well up in his eye. He wiped it on his sleeve and changed the subject to something less painful. "Well, my uncle is coming back from Europe soon. I'll be glad to see him when he gets here. He's been gone two years, but Aunt Ann says he's my guardian if anything happens to her." Tony sighed heavily. "Anyway, she said I could go to the club tonight if I wanted to."

"Hey, man, if you're bummin' we can make it another night."

"No, I'm okay. I do want to get out. It gets to you after a while, seeing her lie there on the couch hoping that some miracle will happen."

"No doubt."

"I'll call Pam and see if she's gonna meet us there," Tony said. "Maybe Cindy will go with her."

"I almost asked her out today."

"Cindy?"

"Yeah, but . . ."

"But you lost your backbone," Tony said finishing Bone's sentence.

"Turned into jelly and slid into my butt," Bone replied. "I swear I'm such a dweeb."

"So what time do you want me to come over?" Tony asked.

"Say seven-thirty."

"Okay. I'll call Pam and see what's up. I'll call you back if Cindy's gonna be there so you can start getting nervous early."

"Thanks, man," Bone said sarcastically.

"No prob," Tony replied.

"See ya."

"Later."

Bone hung up and went into the living room to watch the Ren and Stimpy show that he had recorded last night. He turned on the television and the VCR. He rewound the tape and pressed play. Bone heard the torrid drum beat of the show's theme song and settled back into the chair to watch his favorite show.

As Ren the Chihuahua slapped his smiling dimwitted fat cat partner, Stimpy, Bone began to think about Cindy Macleod and how he might be able to approach her at the Night Owl Club.

Jake Demos stood by the entrance of the Night Owl Club. Demos was a tall thin man with a face like a bird of prey. White hair like a bald eagle. A hooked nose like a hawk. He was the owner of the teen club and somewhat of an enigma to the youths that frequented the place. He spoke little, but there was a tension within him that made them a little uneasy.

"Look at that scene, man," Bone said as he and Tony approached the entrance to the club. "Demos looks like the devil at the gates of hell in front of that place, doesn't he?"

Tony looked at the owner standing under the one blue bulb that lit the doorway of the dark and creepy old building and had to admit that Bone was right. "Yeah, he does."

"Those dead trees are spooky, too," Bone said in a whisper. He stared at the curved black trees that seemed to clutch the building in their grasp. "Look at them. Man, that place must be haunted like they say around town. No wonder they call it the

Nightmare Club"

Tony glanced at the trees.

"Spooky," Bone said. "Real spooky."

Tony nodded. It was a scary-looking place. Maybe what they said about it was true. Maybe there really were ghosts. Maybe . . . Just then, Tony realized that something was crawling on the back of his neck! He yelped and spun around, slapping at his nape.

Bone cracked up as he waved the stick that he had just rubbed across his friend's skin.

"You wad," Tony said, grabbing the stick and swatting Bone on the arm with it.

"Ow, man, chill out," Bone said, still laughing despite the stinging pain in his arm. "You should've seen your face."

Tony shook his head, snapped the stick in half and tossed it. "You're a real jerk, man."

"Evening, gentlemen," Jake Demos said in a quiet voice.

"What's up," Tony said, as he passed the owner and went inside the club.

Demos looked at Bone. His eyes seemed to darken. He smiled. "Welcome to the 'gates of hell,' son."

Bone felt his face flush. He smiled blandly, stepped passed Demos and went inside. He grabbed Tony by the arm. "Hey, did you hear what he just said to me?"

"Yeah, welcome. Why what'd you think he said?"

"He said, 'Welcome to the gates of hell,' " Bone replied.

"Sure, right," Tony shook his head as if Bone were joking around, then started looking for Pam. "I wonder where they are."

28

Bone looked back at the entrance and saw that Demos was gone from the door. He looked around the room and saw the owner standing over by the pool room. "Hey, Tony, look." He pointed over at Demos.

"So?"

"So how'd he get past us?"

"He walked. Now quit kidding around."

Bone sighed, deciding to drop the issue. He must have heard Demos incorrectly and the owner could've passed by them when they were talking.

"Let's go get a table," Tony said.

"Sounds good," Bone said.

They walked across the club, which still had remnants from the Halloween masquerade ball that Ian Montgomery had put on last week. A few scattered cobwebs still hung in the corners of the club.

"I still can't believe those two kids got killed last week," Bone said. "They went to the ball and then they were found dead later."

"That Yvette chick and Michael Roca?"

"Yeah. That was some scary stuff. I didn't know her, but Roca was a pretty cool dude. He was into makeup and movies."

"I guess you never know when your number's up."

"No, but I don't want some psycho helping me along. I prefer to be murdered by old age."

"Yeah, we all would," Tony said thinking of his aunt. "Let's sit down."

They sat at their favorite table in the corner of the main room. The waitress approached their table.

"Can I get you guys something to drink?" Jenny Demos said. She was Jake's daughter and co-owner of the Night Owl Club.

"I'll have a Coke," Tony said.

"No thanks, I have a light," Bone said picking up the lamp on the table and putting it beside the flower on the table. "A 'Bud' light."

Tony groaned. Jenny smiled.

"Okay, so just a Coke," she said, turning to leave.

"And a ginger ale . . . straight up," Bone said, playing the tough guy. "Better yet, make it a double, sister."

Jenny laughed and wrote the order down on a small tablet. "Back in a minute."

Jenny walked back to the snack bar where her dad was pouring drinks from the soda fountain. The snack bar was formerly a regular bar when the Night Owl Club was a speakeasy during prohibition. A couple of teens rested one of their feet on the brass foot rail and scoped the room for babes.

In a few minutes Jenny returned with two drinks. "Dollar fifty," she said.

"Take care of that, would you?" Bone said, with a casual wave of his hand.

Tony shook his head and handed the girl a couple of dollars. She gave him the change back and he handed her a quarter.

"Thanks," Jenny said, then went to wait on the other customers.

"Hey, Pam. Over here!" Tony shouted when he saw his girlfriend looking for them from across the room.

Bone turned and saw Pam and a few of her friends. He felt a butterfly flutter in his stomach when he saw that Cindy Macleod was one of her companions.

"There she is, Bone," Tony said, referring to the pretty blonde. "Your woman."

"I see her, man," Bone replied, shoving his friend's arm.

"Now don't get nervous and wet your pants."

"Just shut up, will you?" Bone said. He started fixing his shirt collar.

Tony laughed at his friend's flustered behavior as the girls approached the table.

"Hey, Pam," Tony said.

"Hi, Tone," Pam said then added, "hi, Bone."

"Hey!" Fenimore said, raising a finger in the air as he tried to dispel his nervousness with his natural defense system—a joke. "That sounds great. Tone and Bone. Sounds like a cop show. I'm Bone, he's Tone, we're cops working the danger zone."

Pam laughed.

"I can see it as a summer replacement on Fox," Bone said.

"I can see you as a summer replacement for someone at the Wakefield mental hospital," Tony said, shaking his head.

"Hi, guys," Cindy said, smiling.

"Hi, Cindy," Tony said, then looked over at Bone.

"Hey," Bone replied, fixing his hair even though it wasn't mussed.

"Hi, Bone."

"Hey, Tony," Mary Kelly, the other girl with Pam, said ignoring Bone whom she despised ever since he put a lizard in her lunch box in sixth grade. She was a chunky sixteen-year-old with spiky hair and a prickly disposition.

31

"Mary, Mary, quite contrary," Bone said, smiling.

"Bite it, Bonehead," she sneered.

The girls and Tony laughed as did Bone who loved to get a reaction out of the stocky brunette.

"What's going on?" Tony said to his girlfriend.

"Nothing," Pam replied as she looked around the room. "It's pretty crowded in here tonight."

The inside of the Night Owl Club was more modern than the outside's dreary appearance. Much of the ground floor had been converted into a combo dance floor, game room, and snack bar. Music blared from the jukebox that stood against the wall. Kids danced in slashing rays of light reflected from the faceted glass ball that hung over the dance floor. An arched doorway led to the game room where spirited games of fooz ball, pool, video games, and air hockey took place nightly.

"Hey, there's Kevin," Mary said when she saw the blond-haired, blue-eyed jock. She called out to him, "Hey, Kevin! Come here!"

Mary knew that Kevin Court liked Cindy. She also suspected that Bone Fenimore liked her friend as well. She had seen the way her lifelong antagonist had looked at Cindy when she had approached the table and recognized the symptoms of puppy love.

Kevin Court approached the table. He was a handsome seventeen-year-old, a pretty good athlete and, much to Bone's chagrin, a pretty nice guy.

"Hey, guys," Kevin said.

"Hi, Kevin."

"Kevin."

"Hey."

"Bone man, Bull Merritt was talking about you at practice this afternoon," Kevin said to Fenimore.

"Really? You can understand his grunts?" Bone said and everyone laughed.

"Yeah," Kevin said. "Him and Truck came late. I guess they went after you after school?"

"Yeah, they did, but I blew them off."

"That's what Truck said."

"So is Merritt still after Bone?" Tony asked.

Kevin nodded and looked at Fenimore, "Bull said he's gonna kick your tail."

"Seems like he was the one with the tail," Bone said.

Again the group laughed.

"I'd watch out if I were you," Kevin said.

"I'm looking for an eye donor right now so I can get an extra set of peepers put in the back of my head."

The group cracked up. Bone was on a roll.

"Kevin, are you here with anybody?" Mary asked, trying to break up Bone's comic rhythm while at the same time play matchmaker for Kevin with Cindy.

"Yeah, Jimmy Carrington, but he's out dancing with some chick from the riding academy."

"Where are you sitting?"

"Nowhere. We're just kinda roaming."

"Oh. Well, why don't you guys sit with us?" Mary said, smiling broadly as she looked over at Bone.

"Hey, Mary, I like your new hairdo," Bone said in rebuttal. He knew that Mary was provoking him. "Is that Paul Mitchell or Spike Lee? Oh, I know, you're going to play a cactus in the school play."

Cindy and Pam tried not to laugh at their friend,

but they couldn't help letting a giggle escape. Mary's hairstyle was a bit extreme.

"You're a real dork, Bonehead," Mary said.

"Ooh, good comeback," Bone said. "I think those spikes must have grown inward and poked holes in your brain."

"A real dork," Mary reiterated.

Tony laughed. "Okay, round one's over. Come on, guys."

The song on the jukebox changed to the latest rap from Arrested Development.

"Oh, that's my favorite song, Pam said, starting to move to the groove in her chair.

"You want to dance?" Tony asked, picking up her cue.

"Let's go," Pam said.

A moment later, a guy with a brush hair cut came over and asked Mary to dance. She accepted and went to the dance floor with the cadet from Hudson Academy.

Bone was thinking about asking Cindy to dance when Kevin got up from his chair.

"Let's dance," Kevin said as he took Cindy by the hand. She smiled, glanced at Bone, then got up to dance.

Bone felt left out as he looked at the dance floor and saw everyone dancing. He felt a nervous jump in his gut when he saw Cindy smiling and dancing with Kevin. It should be him out there, not Kevin Court. If only he wasn't so afraid of being rejected.

Unable to stand it, Bone got up from the table and started to wander around the club. He went into the game room, played one game of "Mash the Monkey," got bored, and left.

The song changed from fast and funky to slow and romantic. Bone looked out on the dance floor and saw Pam and Tony dancing cheek to cheek. He also saw Cindy and Kevin holding each other close as they swayed to the music. Bone felt his ears burn and a sick feeling in his stomach.

"Way to go, Bonehead," he whispered and continued roaming into a deserted section of the club.

Curious, he decided to explore. He entered a dark room that looked like a storeroom of some kind. Big cobwebs hung in the corners and a stale smell tinged the air. The music seemed to stop and die in the stillness. Bone had to admit that it was a little creepy in the room by himself, but watching Cindy dance with Kevin was worse.

On the far wall of the storeroom, he saw a polished wooden door with a bare bulb shining above it. The new door looked out of place in the ancient looking storeroom, so Bone decided to do a little investigating. He moved to the door, opened it, then stepped through it.

In the light from the bulb over the door, Bone could make out a stairwell below him. It was dimly lit and didn't look like it had been used for some time.

"Jeez, check it out," Bone whispered.

He took a cautious step onto the first step. It felt solid, but creaked eerily in the silence.

For a moment, fear tapped Bone on the shoulder with a skeletal finger. Maybe it wasn't such a good idea to go down into the basement of a place that was supposed to be haunted. The stairwell looked like the kind of place that the stupid hero in a horror movie went as the audience shouted for him to stay out. He looked back at the door and almost started to head back to the main room.

But then he thought about having to watch his would-be girlfriend dancing the night away with the football player while he sat there trying to be the funny guy.

He turned back around and took another cautious creaky step. This one also felt firm. Slowly, he made his way down the stairs.

At the midpoint, the stairs stopped and there was a platform. To the right was a door. It seemed odd to Bone that a door would appear in the middle of the stairs, but there it was.

I'd like to meet the dude who designed this place some time, Bone thought.

He took a step toward the door and heard music coming from inside. A cold wind from the gap at the bottom of the door blew past his feet. Startled, he took a step backward. The music seemed to grow louder. He heard laughter. It sounded like *someone* was having a good time. He looked down the stairs into the darkness and decided that his exploration of the Nightmare Club had ended for the night. He would check out what was happening behind the door. He took a step forward, grabbed the cold knob, turned it, opened the door, and stepped inside the room.

* * *

"Where'd the Bone man go?" Kevin asked as he and Cindy joined Tony and Pam back at the table.

"I dunno." Tony said, looking around the room. "He was here when we started dancing."

"That was so funny when he was ragging on Mary," Cindy said with a giggle. "Her hair is kinda crunchy."

"Bone knows how to get to people when he wants to," Tony said.

"Yeah, he's gonna joke himself into a hospital bed if he keeps doing stuff like hanging tails on Bull Merritt," Kevin said.

"That was kind of dumb. Why does he do stuff like that?" Cindy asked Tony.

"Why does he tell the teachers crazy stories that he makes up and get in trouble? It's just Bone being the Funny Bone," Tony replied.

Pam giggled. "I remember the time he got you with that necklace."

Tony rolled his eyes. "He didn't *get* me. I knew he was kidding."

Pam laughed. "No way. He got you good, and you know it."

"He got me . . . *Not.*"

"What are you guys talking about?" Cindy said. "I never heard this one before."

"It's nothing," Tony said. "Just something Bone did a couple of years ago."

"What'd he do, Pam?"

Pam smiled. "Can I tell her?"

Tony waved his hand. "I'll tell her."

"So what was it?" Cindy asked.

"Well, I had just met Bone in history class, and we

started hanging. After a couple of days, he saw me in the gym after school. And he came up to me with this real serious look on his face. I mean really serious."

Pam laughed, anticipating the story.

Tony continued, "So Bone says, 'I have something to tell you.' and he's got this look. Real serious. So then he hands me this little box. I open it and inside is this little charm shaped like a leg bone and it's on a necklace. I got this weird feeling in my gut when I saw it and the way he was looking at me."

Confused, Cindy shook her head. "So what'd he say?"

"He told me that ever since he saw me in class he'd had a crush on me. Man, I almost choked when he said that. Then he tried to grab my hand. I drew back to hit him and then he started laughing like crazy."

"And you knew he got you," Pam said.

Tony nodded. "Yeah, he got me. I did freak a little. He played it so perfect."

"You still have the necklace and charm?" Cindy asked. "I would've tossed it in the trash."

Tony pulled the charm out from under his shirt. "Yeah. I wear it as a reminder to never fall for one of Fenimore's jokes. So far it's worked pretty well."

"Are you sure that's why you keep it," Pam said. "You guys are pretty close. Maybe you've got something going."

"Now who's the comedian?" Tony said, rolling his eyes.

Cindy laughed.

"Hey, Cin, you want to dance again?" Kevin said.

"No, I think I'll sit out for a while."

Kevin was disapppointed.

"I wonder if Bone left," Tony said, scanning the club again.

"He's probably thinking of some joke to play on us."

"Yeah, that's his idea of a fun night," Tony said.

Pam smiled. "And what's your idea?"

Tony's eyes met hers.

"Well, if we go outside, maybe I can think of something."

Pam smiled.

"We'll be back in a little bit," Tony said, forgetting all about his friend.

The room was much larger than Bone expected and much more interesting. Twin spotlights shone on a silver mirrored globe that hung from the ceiling and reflected the light in strange and wonderful streams around the room. The beams of light cut white paths through a haze of smoke that floated through the room. It fell onto the faces of the teenagers that filled the room. Bone didn't recognize any of the kids and figured that they must be from the Cooper Riding Academy for Girls or Hudson Military Academy. He wondered how they managed to smoke cigarettes here when Demos didn't allow it.

As he took a step inside, Bone noticed that the mist had a sweet, soothing smell, not the harsh odor of burning tobacco. Bone took a deep breath and felt relaxed. He looked at the teens again and saw that none were smoking. The mist must have been generated from some hidden smoke machine.

The hard driving beat of the music thumped against Bone. He watched the kids dancing on the wooden floor and was struck by how well they all moved. Every one of them was really great. Immediately, he crossed out the possibility that he might ask a girl to dance with him. Bone always felt that he had the rhythm of an epileptic drummer and having to dance among this group of would-be Star Searchers was sure to make him feel like he had two left feet sewn on backward.

"Hey, Bone, what's up?" a male voice said.

Bone turned and saw a stocky teenager coming toward him. He didn't recognize the guy.

"Hey," Bone said hesitantly.

"Come on in, man," the smiling teen said, gesturing with his hand in a friendly fashion.

"Do I know you?" Bone asked, stepping further into the room.

"Bob, Bob Wisniski, Cooper High."

The teen shook Bone's hand.

"How do you know me?" Bone asked. "I don't remember seeing you at school."

"Are you kidding? Everybody knows Funny Bone Fenimore."

Bone smiled. It felt good to be recognized.

Bob continued, "A friend told me what you did today with the tail and then the story you told Mr. Kitchens about the aliens. Choice stuff, man."

Bone laughed. "It was pretty funny."

"Pretty funny? Hilarious is what it was," Bob turned and shouted to a guy sitting at a candlelit table across the room, "Hey, Jackie, look who just came in. Bone Fenimore."

Bone looked over and saw a handsome teenager look his way and wave.

"Come on over," Jackie said, as he beckoned Bone and Bob to come over to the table.

As he walked toward the table, Bone tried to place the two teenagers, but came up blank. Oh well, he thought, I can't know all my fans.

"Hey, Bone," Jackie said, extending his hand. Bone shook it.

"What's up, uh, Jackie, right?"

"Yeah, Jackie Pressman. Have a seat, Bone." Jackie smiled.

"I was just telling Bone how funny he was today with the tail and alien stuff," Bob said.

"Oh yeah, man, that was choice."

"I'm glad you guys liked it."

"Funny."

Bone looked around the room. "Man, I didn't even know about this part of the club."

Jackie smiled broadly. "It's the best, man, the absolute best. The best-looking chicks always come to this room. In fact, I think I see one looking my way. Excuse me, boys, while I make my move."

Jackie got up and walked over to the next table and asked a pretty blond girl to dance. She accepted. Bone watched them go out onto the dance floor. It was then he noticed that there *were* a lot of good-looking girls in the room. In fact, most of the people in the room were what he called "Stuckons." They were so good-looking that they were usually *stuck on* themselves.

But these kids didn't seem to be that way. He looked at a couple of girls who smiled and waved to him. He looked away, embarrassed by the attention, but it did make him feel a tingle of butterflies in his stomach. One of the girls got up and came over to the table. Bone thought she must know Bob, but she came right over to him.

"Hi," the girl said.

"Hi," Bone replied.

"You're the guy they call Funny Bone, aren't you?"

"Geez, I must be wearing a sign tonight."

"Well, you are, aren't you?" She asked, smiling.

"I was when I came in here. Unless somebody switched bodies with me."

The girl laughed. "I'm Ashley."

"Hi Ashley, and it's Bone, Funny Bone is my formal name," Bone said amazed at how easily the words came. Usually, upon meeting a pretty girl, his brain and his mouth disconnected.

"You must be a pretty funny guy to get a nickname like that," she said.

"I've gotten a few laughs before," Bone said, proud of his reputation.

Ashley smiled.

"So do you go to Cooper, too?" Bone asked.

"I used to."

"Oh, did you move or something?"

"Sort of."

She looked away and Bone realized he must have touched on a sensitive subject. He quickly changed it. "So how do you know me? I mean, you're the third person who's known me and I haven't known them."

"I saw you around school and asked my friend who you were."

"I thought you said you didn't go to Cooper."

"I don't. I have friend that goes there."

"Oh."

What the hell are you doing giving her the third degree, stupid? Bone asked himself. The first time a girl actually comes up and starts talking to you and you have to play Sherlock Holmes.

Ashley didn't seem to notice. She smiled. "I asked her who the cute guy with the deep brown eyes was and she told me."

"Oh, uh, my friend Tony says they're brown because I'm full of bull," Bone said, joking his way around the compliment. "The funny guy" comment he could handle, but "the cute guy?" He took a deep breath of the sweet mist and felt better.

"Did you get those eyes from your mom or your dad?" Ashley said, still smiling.

"Both I think. See they got together one cold night and well, you know the rest," Bone said diffusing the compliment with his self-deprecating humor again.

Ashley laughed. "You're not too good at taking a compliment, are you?"

A voice interrupted the girl's question.

"Hey, Bone, you want a Coke or something?" Bob asked as he got up. "Oh, hey, Ashley," the stocky boy said, noticing the girl for the first time.

"Hey, Bob," Ashley said, annoyed by the interruption.

"No, I'm cool," Bone answered.

Bone took another breath of the misty air and

looked over at the pretty girl with whom he was sitting. She met his eyes and smiled warmly.

The music changed from fast to slow.

"Ashley, would you like to dance?" Bone said almost without realizing it. He saw the look of surprise on her face and immediately wished he could take it back. It was practically an unwritten rule that a guy should fast dance with a girl before he slow danced with her.

"Sure," she said. "I'd like that."

Bone didn't move. He was sure that she had turned him down, "Well, maybe the next one."

Ashley smiled. "I said, *yes,* now come on."

She took Bone's hand and led him out to the dance floor.

"I guess Bone went home," Tony said to Pam as they went back into the club.

The two teenagers had been making out in Tony's van until their passion overcame them and they had to stop before things went further than either wanted. Pam had pledged to keep her virginity intact until she was sure that her relationship was based on love and respect not just passion and hormones. She realized that Tony was very special and she loved him a lot, but sometimes she felt that he was holding something back from her. She had even asked him a few times how he felt about their relationship, but he always skirted the issue. When Pam pressed him for an answer, he would get sulky. She thought it might have something to do with his parents' untimely deaths and his aunt's illness, but she couldn't be sure since Tony didn't talk about either subject in great detail.

"What time is it?" Tony said.

"Late. I have to go to," Pam said, looking at her watch and seeing that it was approaching eleven-thirty.

Tony looked out toward the dance floor and saw Kevin and Cindy dancing. "I thought you said Cindy didn't like Kevin."

"That's what she told me. Why? You wanna go out with her?"

"Yeah, she's my dream date," Tony answered, sarcastically.

"So what do you care?"

"Well, Bone sort of likes her."

"Bone?" Pam said, grinning incredulously. Never before had she imagined Bone with a girl much less her friend, Cindy. The idea was, well, funny to her. "You're talking about Bone Fenimore?"

"You know I am."

"Bone Fenimore? Skinny guy? Always playing jokes? Never serious? That Bone Fenimore?"

"What's wrong with that?"

"I just can't picture him with Cindy that's all."

"What? She's too cool for him," Tony said, getting a little ticked off at her attitude toward his friend.

Pam caught his anger and shot it right back at him. "That's not what I said."

"Well, what do you mean? Bone's not an ug."

"I know. But I've never seen him serious about anything. I just can't see him with a girl like Cindy or any girl for that matter."

45

"So because he's funny, he should be a comedian monk or something?"

"No, I just, never mind," Pam sighed, tired of arguing, "if Bone wants to ask her out, why doesn't he?"

"He's shy."

"Oh, he hangs a tail on the meanest guy in school and he's shy."

"Around girls. Maybe you could hint around and see if Cindy might go out with him."

Pam looked out on the floor and saw Kevin kissing Cindy. "I think it's too late."

Tony saw the kiss and frowned.

Pam saw his disappointment. "I wouldn't worry about it. You know Cindy. A kiss doesn't mean much."

"I guess. I just hope Bone *did* go home. I don't want him to get hurt seeing her out there kissing Kevin."

"Well, I'm sure he's gone. He's not anywhere in here," Pam said, "And where else could he be?"

Tony shrugged. He had no idea of the fate of his friend.

Bone felt Ashley's soft hair brush his neck, and he shivered. The sixteen-year-old felt like he was dancing on air. They had been on the dance floor for a long time. After the first slow song ended, Ashley convinced Bone to stay on the floor to fast dance with her. He did and danced like he had never danced. They were the stars on the floor and a couple of times people stopped just to watch them. Bone loved every minute of it. At the end of a set of jamming tunes, a slow song drifted out of the speakers. The soft music was a wave and he and Ashley floated on it. Bone didn't recognize the song. It was one he had never heard before, but it was great for slow dancing.

"You're an awesome dancer," Ashley whispered in Bone's ear. Her warm breath sent another shiver dancing up his spine.

"Thanks," Bone replied feeling twenty feet tall.

He looked around the dance floor and saw that he and Ashley were the only ones on it again.

The song seemed to go on forever. When it finally ended, Bone felt both exhilarated and drained at the same time. He held Ashley's hand as they went back to the table.

The two guys were gone. In fact the place had thinned out considerably. Bone glanced at his watch.

"What?" he exclaimed.

He looked again.

"No way."

He looked for a third time, but the dial didn't change. It was two-thirty in the morning. He was supposed to have been home two and a half hours ago!

"What's wrong?" Ashley asked.

"It—it's two-thirty. I have to go, Ashley," Bone stammered. "My dad'll kill me for being so late."

"But we were just getting to know each other."

"I—I know. Listen. Tomorrow's Saturday night. You want to, uh, you want to go out with me?" If I can, he thought dismally as he looked at his watch.

"I can't."

Bone's stomach lurched. Why had he rushed it?

47

"I understand. I shouldn't have . . ."

"No, I want to. But I already told my friends I'd meet them here."

"Oh."

Lame excuse, Bone thought.

"I know it sounds like a lame excuse, but you could meet me here tomorrow night."

Bone didn't ponder her coincidental choice of words. He only answered. "Yeah, that'd be great."

"Then I'll see you tomorrow?"

"Yeah. What time?"

"Anytime after dark."

"Oh, okay. Now I better get home before my dad turns me into a pumpkin."

Ashley smiled as she looked into his eyes and then at his lips. Bone felt himself melt. "I'll see you," he said, missing Ashley's cue that she wanted him to kiss her good night.

As Bone left and got outside the room, he suddenly felt woozy. He staggered on the steps for a moment and then regained his balance. He wondered why Jake Demos hadn't come down and told the teens in the room that the place was closed. The Night Owl Club always closed at midnight. Just then, a thought struck him. What if the doors were locked? What if he couldn't get out of the club until the next morning? Oh, man, his dad would kill him. He rushed up the stairs and stepped into the darkened club upstairs. There was no one around and a sinking feeling dipped in his stomach. He just knew that the door would be locked. He took a step when he heard a noise come from behind him. He turned and saw a phantom figure step out from the darkened shadows of the room. For a moment, Bone was frightened until he saw the white hair of Jake Demos reflected in a faint shaft of light.

"What are you doing in here?" Jake asked. His voice sounded different in the silence of the room. It was eerie.

"I was downstairs. I didn't hear you say it was time to go."

"Well, go on home. The door's open."

Bone nodded and hurried to the door. When he got outside, he suddenly remembered that Tony had driven him to the club.

"Oh, man," he groaned as if things couldn't get any worse. He started to walk for home. He wished he would've brought a heavier jacket. The night air was cold and he anticipated a long miserable walk to his house.

"Need a ride?"

Bone turned and again saw the shadowy figure of Jake Demos—this time standing outside the door to the club. "Oh, man, could you? I'm already in big trouble."

"I know," Jake said with a touch of amusement in his voice. "Come on."

Demos moved out of the doorway and into the parking lot. he walked over to a Porsche and beckoned Bone to get into the vehicle. Bone did, and they were soon on the road. The winding curves of Thirteen Bends Road were not advantageous to speed, but Demos skillfully negotiated them as he pressed the accelerator to the floor. Bone didn't mind the speed since he was in a hurry to get home.

"Thanks a lot," Bone said, "I sure appreciate the ride."

"I know," Demos replied.

As they passed under a lone street lamp, Bone glanced at Demos and was shocked. For a moment, his face seemed to change. It appeared to thicken. His jowls seemed heavier. His white hair darkened.

"What's the matter?" Demos said, sensing Bone's distress.

"Oh, uh, nothing," Bone said as he looked into the cold eyes of the thin man and saw no evidence of a change in appearance. The teenager convinced himself that the transformation must've been a trick of the shifting light and fatigue caused by the lateness of the hour.

They continued the drive down Thirteen Bends Road until they got to the intersection of Thirteen Bends and Old Wilson Highway.

"Turn . . ." Bone said, as Demos made the correct turn before the teen finished, "right here."

Without further directions Jake drove right to the Fenimores' house and parked. Bone couldn't imagine how Demos knew just where to go, but he wasn't going to question it now. Bone was simply glad to be home.

"Thanks a lot, Mr. Demos."

Demos nodded.

"I'll see you tomorrow night," Demos said as Bone grabbed the doorhandle and popped open the door.

"Yeah, uh, okay."

How did he know that I would be coming back tomorrow night? Bone wondered before deciding that it was a lucky guess. Most kids went to the Night Owl Club on Saturday nights. Besides he was probably just trying to drum up business.

So why am I starting to get the chills? Bone asked himself as he got out of the car.

"Goodbye," Demos said.

"See ya and thanks again," the teenager said, looking into the car.

Demos nodded and put the sports car in gear.

Bone waved as the Porsche sped away. He looked toward the house, swallowed, and went to the front door. He unlocked it and stepped inside the foyer. Hurriedly, he went down the hallway past the living room.

"Hold it," said a deep voice.

Bone turned the corner and saw his father sitting in the eerie blue glow cast by the television.

"A little late, aren't we?" asked Bone's dad.

"Yeah, a little." Bone grinned.

"Excuse?"

"I met this hot-looking girl and we were slow dancing and when I looked at my watch it was 2:30."

Bone's dad nodded. "Right. You and a hot-looking girl. Why do I find that hard to believe?"

"I swear."

"Unh huh. Well, you can stay home for a couple of days until you tell me the truth."

"Oh, man, I swear it's true."

"Any more lip and it'll be a week."

Bone bit his tongue and turned around. Suddenly he remembered his semi-date with Ashley. He had

51

told her that they would meet tomorrow night. And now he was on restriction.

"Dad, please I can't stay home tomorrow night. I have a date."

"You really must want a week's restriction."

"Dad."

"Go to bed, Harold. Now."

Bone clicked his tongue and turned on his heel. Disgusted, he tromped up the stairs. Maybe he could plead his case with his mom in the morning. Sometimes he could get her to change his dad's mind for him.

When he got to his room, Bone shed his clothes. His shirt still held the scent of the mist in the room. It reminded him of Ashley and a smile crept on his face, but it disappeared when he heard his father's footsteps coming up the stairs.

After brushing his teeth in the bathroom, Bone came back to his room and climbed into bed. He turned off the light, then closed his eyes and saw Ashley's face. Smiling, he drifted off to dreamland.

Two

The phone rang, waking Bone from a fitful sleep. He reached over, and grabbed the handset and put it to his ear. But before he could say anything, he heard his mother answering the extension.

"Hello, Mrs. Fenimore, how are you?" Tony asked.

"Fine. Bone's asleep. You boys stayed out a little too late last night, didn't you?"

"Oh, I was home at midnight."

"Oh?"

"I got it, Mom," Bone said, his voice creaky with sleep.

"Bye, Mrs. Fenimore."

"Goodbye, Tony."

Bone's mom hung up, but Bone knew she would be asking him where he was last night.

"Hey, dude, where'd you go last night?" Tony asked his friend.

"I went to a room in another part of the club."

"What room?"

"I don't know what they call it. It's halfway down a set of stairs in the back part of the club. I went in and met this girl. We danced all night — until two-thirty in

53

the morning."

"Yeah, right," Tony said. "You met a girl and danced all night. Where'd you *really* go?"

"I swear. Her name's Ashley and she's a fox."

Tony laughed. "Man, you went to a room in the middle of some stairs where you met a foxy babe. You can do better than that."

"Man, I'm not kidding. We danced fast and slow. People watched us we were so good."

"Oh, all of a sudden, you're dancing with some foxy babe. Come on, Bone, you're not getting me with that stuff."

"All right, don't believe me. I'll take you to the room tonight." Suddenly, Bone remembered his little problem. "Oh, man, I forgot."

Tony smiled. "Oh, what'd you conveniently forget?"

"You're a wad sometimes," Bone said.

"So what'd you forget?" Tony asked, again.

"I got put on restriction. My dad caught me coming in last night and got pissed."

"So you can't take me to this room tonight?" Tony said, smugly secure in the belief that Bone was pulling his leg.

"I swear I'm not kidding."

"I know you're not," Tony said.

"Man, I'm gonna sneak out tonight and show you. You can even meet Ashley. We're supposed to get together again tonight."

"I can't wait. How you gonna sneak out?"

"I'll go out the window of my room."

"And jump down from two stories?"

"Yeah."

"Well, don't waste your time. I've got to stay home with my aunt tonight. She's real bad this morning."

"That's bummin'."

"Yeah."

Tony paused and then changed the subject back to Bone's story about the room at the club where he danced with the foxy babe. "So you're not gonna tell me where you really went last night?"

Bone knew Tony wasn't going to believe him so he just shook his head and said, "I changed into a were-wolf and killed a couple of sheep and an old shephard."

"That's more believable."

"Funny," Bone said.

"Oh, hey, I gotta go. Aunt Ann's calling." Tony said, abruptly.

"Okay."

"Are you really on restriction? I was calling you to come over and shoot some hoops."

"Yeah, I am. I told you . . ."

"Right, you and the babe dancing till two-thirty." Tony heard his aunt call him again. "I gotta go."

"See you."

"Later."

Tony hung up.

Bone dropped the phone on the hook and laid down on the bed to think. He needed a plan to get to the Night Owl Club tonight. If only he had gotten Ashley's phone number, he could call her and tell her that he couldn't make it. But since he didn't get her number, he *had* to find a way to get to the club without getting caught. Otherwise, she might think he was blowing her off. He had to figure out a plan.

Bone spent the day trying to come up with a plan to get him out of the house undetected. His answer came while he was watching an old episode of "Spies Like Us." In it, the hero, Kensington Slade, escaped by tying some sheets to the foot of the bed and lowering himself to the ground.

Bone went into the garage, got his dad's hundred foot long heavy duty extension cord and smuggled it to his bedroom. The cord was thick and strong, yet supple enough to tie. He would secure it to the foot of his bed, toss it out the window and climb down.

Bone decided that nine o'clock would be the best time for him to make his escape. His mom would be watching her favorite show and his dad more than likely would be asleep on the couch. He could slip out then without much of a chance of being caught. But how was he going to get to the club? His bike was still in sad shape from the encounter with Bull and Truck. The idea of hitchhiking was out. If one of his parent's friends saw him, he would get into real trouble. So how to get there? Tony was staying home with his aunt, but maybe another of his friends could take him. Or he could borrow a bike. Then, suddenly, it came to him.

"My blades." Bone said, as he recalled the in-line skates that he had gotten for his birthday. He could skate to the club and then hide the blades in the bushes so that he wouldn't look like a geek carrying them around with him. It wasn't that far away, and he was pretty good on the skates. He figured it might take a half hour to get there so if he left at nine that would get him there at nine-thirty. That was about the same time that he'd met Ashley last night so the escape plan timetable worked out perfectly.

The plan sounded good, but something was still nagging him. What was he forgetting?

Oh, right. What if Mom or Dad looks in on him?

The answer came quickly. No problem. He would put his quilt under his covers and shape it to look like his body. If they looked into the room, they would think he was in bed asleep.

So now he *really* had his plan. All he had to do was wait until the zero hour and then implement it.

Nine o'clock rolled around and Bone was dressed in his loose-fitting jeans, New York Giants sweatshirt and Reeboks. When he saw his reflection in the mirror, he sighed, feeling like a skinny dork trying to look cool. He combed his hair for the fifth time, but it wasn't cooperating. He glanced at the clock. Time to go. Oh, well, it's dark in the room so maybe she won't notice the unruly hair.

He put the quilt on the bed, shaped it into a close approximation of his body, then covered it with his blankets. He stepped back and admired his work. He had to admit it did look as though someone was sleeping in the bed.

Satisfied with the deception, Bone went to the closet and got his in-line skates. He spun the wheels to make sure everything was in working order then walked over to the window. He put the blades into a knapsack on the floor at his feet and opened the window. He pulled out the screen and set it against the wall. Reaching down, he picked up the sack and tossed it out of the window to the ground. He took the extension cord from under the bed and tied it to the foot of the heavy frame. He tugged on the cord to tighten the knot then checked it. It felt secure. He turned off the light in his room and carried the remainder of the extension cord over to the window. When he tossed it out, the cord uncoiled before hitting the ground. Again, Bone tugged on the cord to make sure it was secure.

"Oh well, it's time, Kensington. Let's do it," Bone said softly.

Crawling onto the window sill, he grabbed the rope and started to climb down the side of the house. Exactly one step into his descent, it happened.

The knot on the cord came apart.

"Whoah Shhht," Bone said, falling toward the ground trying to keep his feet under him. When he hit the grass feet first, he rolled to absorb the shock and felt his butt land on one of the skates. A shaft of pain lanced his rump as the hard sole and a set of rollers dug into his flesh. His elbow also throbbed from hitting the ground in the fall.

Bone was still for a minute looking up into the sky before standing up to access the damage. He took a couple of steps. His right ankle twinged with pain, but it wasn't bad. His butt was sore, but it would fade. He checked his elbow and found a black smear

58

of dirt.

"Oh, man," he said, more upset with the dirt on his nice shirt than his aching butt, but there was nothing he could do about either of them now.

Bone gathered up the extension cord and hid it in the bushes beside the house. Then he went to the sidewalk and took the skates out of his sack. He took off his shoes and slipped them into the knapsack, put on his skates, and stood. He tested his ankle. It was fine, so he pushed off and was on his way.

After arriving at the club, Bone skated over to a clump of bushes. He changed his skates for his shoes again, slipped the sack with the skates into the bushes, then walked into the club.

The first thing he did was look around for Ashley among the crowd of kids. He didn't see her.

Unfortunately, he missed someone else, too. He didn't see Bull Merritt watching him from the pool room.

She must be in the room downstairs, Bone thought as he headed for the back of the club and the staircase that led to the room. He climbed down the stairs and, just like last night, heard music coming from beyond the door to the room. He smiled and went inside.

"Bone!" Bob Wisniski shouted when he saw Bone.

Bone waved. "What's up?"

"Hey, Ashley, Bone's here," Bob called out.

Bone smiled when he saw the pretty girl sitting at a table. She was alone. He figured her friends must be out dancing.

"Hey, Bone," she said, as she waved him over.

"Hi, Ashley," Bone said sitting down next to her and breathing in the sweet-smelling haze.

"How are you tonight?" she asked.

"Great. Except I had a little fall," Bone said, then explained his ill-fated escape from the second-story window.

"You did all that just to keep our date? I'm flattered."

Bone smiled. "Yeah, I even got all this dirt on my clothes—just for you."

Bone held up his arm and showed her the sleeve of his shirt. He was surprised to see that it was clean. "Uh, I guess, hmm." He didn't have an answer as to why the shirt was now spotless.

Ashley took his hand. "I love the way the light hits your eyes."

"The eyes are the windows to the soul," Bone said, with Shakespearean relish then laughed.

Ashley looked strange for a moment as if he'd said something to offend her.

"Hey, I didn't mean to make fun. I just . . ."

Bone felt a hard hand slap him on the shoulder.

"Hey, watch it," Bone said, as he turned to see who was there.

"Watch what, dipwad?" Bull Merritt sneered.

Bone saw the big fullback standing next to him, and his stomach turned.

"Watch what, I asked you, dipwad," Merritt said, pushing Bone slightly.

"Come on, man, why can't you leave me alone?" Bone asked.

"I still owe you."

"I said I was sorry for what I did. Can't you just let it go?"

Bull shook his head. "No way, dipwad. I don't forget a can of paint in my face."

"Who is this jerk?" Ashley said.

Bone felt his stomach lurch as his girlfriend provoked the big football player.

"What'd you call me?" Bull said.

"A jerk," Ashley said, coolly.

For a moment, Bull was taken aback. He rubbed his eyes and looked at this girl again. He thought for a moment she had changed.

"You let your girlfriend do your fighting?" Bull asked, focusing on Bone again.

Bone took a deep breath. A feeling of anger began to bubble inside him.

"Well, do you?" Bull asked, shoving Bone off his chair.

Bone took another deep breath of the sweet-smelling mist.

"Well?" Bull shoved him again.

Suddenly, Bone felt his ears burn. He clenched his jaw. Something snapped inside him.

Bull grinned. He taunted Bone, "You gettin' mad, dipwah—"

Suddenly, Bone's fist smashed Bull square in the face. The sound of his nose crunching seemed louder than the music. Bone swung again. He caught Bull in the cheekbone. The flesh split and blood flowed. The enraged boy lashed out with a kick to the big kid's knee and drove Bull to the floor. Bone jumped on top

61

of him and started punching him in the face. Bull could do nothing, but try to protect himself. Bone was a madman. He punched and cursed as he assaulted his tormentor.

Merritt screamed. "Stop, man, I quit."

Bone kept hitting him.

"Please stop," Merritt whimpered as a blow thumped against his ear.

"Bone, he's had enough," Ashley said, calmly.

Bone stopped and quickly got up off the fullback. Blood dripped from Merritt's nose and the cut in his cheek.

Bull staggered to his feet.

"Get the hell out of here!" Bone shouted out of breath from his efforts. "Just get out!"

Merritt nodded and stumbled toward the door. He turned to see if Bone was following him and his face went white. Some of the teenagers in the room seemed to be almost transparent. Something was wrong. One of the girls had no eyes, just sockets. A boy's blond hair seemed to be moving.

"You hurt me, man! I can't see right," Bull shouted as he stared at the kids in the room. "You messed up my eyes."

"Get out, Merritt," Bone said. "You deserved it."

Bull looked once more and blinked. Now the kids seemed to be normal. He wiped at his blood-stained shirt and staggered out of the room.

"You'll be sorry," Bull mumbled as he disappeared into the shadows of the stairwell.

"Man, you dogged him, Bone," Bob said, as his friend, Jackie, joined him at Bone's side.

"Yeah, you kicked his butt good," Jackie added.

"He . . . deserved . . . it," Bone huffed as his exertions caught up with him. He began to feel a little queasy.

"You were great," Ashley said, as she kissed Bone on the cheek.

Bone felt better.

"Take a few deep breaths," Jackie said. "You're probably lightheaded and need some air."

Bone nodded and took the boy's suggestion. He gulped in a few deep breaths. The smell of the room was almost too sweet. He felt like he was going to barf, but the sudden nausea passed quickly. In fact, after a few more breaths, he felt great. He wasn't winded at all. As he returned to normal, he was able to consider what had just happened. And what had just happened was that he had just beaten Bull Merritt in a fight!

"Bone, you were totally awesome," Ashley said, kissing him again.

"He deserved it." Bone repeated.

"Yeah, he did," Bob agreed.

As Bone took a napkin and wiped the blood off his hands, another girl came up to him and put her hand on his shoulder. "I saw what happened, Bone, you were excellent."

Bone turned to this new girl and smiled sheepishly. He looked over at Ashley expecting her to be jealous. But she just looked at the other girl and smiled.

The girl was a little shorter than Bone. She had curly red hair and the prettiest blue eyes Bone had ever seen.

"I'm Lori," she said, smiling.

"Hi, Lori," Bone said. He was amazed at how good he felt. In the one fight he'd had in his life prior to this one, he remembered that after it was over his whole body was shaky and he felt sick for an hour. But after the fight with Merritt, he felt absolutely great.

"Hey, Lori," Ashley said.

"Hey, Ash."

"So, Ashley, are you gonna share this guy tonight or hog him like you did last night?"

Bone couldn't believe his ears. Lori must have been watching them last night and wanting to dance with him. Tony will never believe this, he thought.

Ashley smiled. "We can share."

Bone couldn't help but grin. Both of the girls were better looking than he could've possibly imagined. Suddenly, he realized that a slow dance was playing and Lori was leading him onto the dance floor. As they started to dance, Bone felt like a king.

Once again, Bone danced the night away, dancing first with Ashley and then Lori. Sometimes on fast songs he danced with them both. The strange thing was that they didn't seem to care. They were perfectly content to share him — and he was perfectly content to be shared.

After the dance, Bone looked at his watch. It was one o'clock in the morning. He frowned.

"What's wrong?" Lori asked.

"I've got to get going."

"Why? Your mom and dad don't know you're out," Lori replied.

Bone looked at her with curiosity. "How do you know that?"

A smiling Ashley interjected, "I told Lori that you got in real late last night."

Lori nodded. "I just figured that you'd be put on restriction. I mean, my mom and dad would've restricted me."

Bone nodded. "Good guess. You guys must be the new Cagney and Lacy."

"Who?" Lori asked.

"The lady cops on that TV show. Remember?"

Neither had ever heard of the show. Ashley changed the subject. "Bone, are you coming to the club Monday night?"

"Monday night?"

"What's wrong with that?"

"It's a school night."

"So?" Ashley said with a smirk.

"So my parents wouldn't like me going out on a school night especially after just getting off restriction."

"My parents don't care."

"Yeah, well, mine do. I can't make it," Bone said, "but I was thinking that maybe we could get together before then. Why don't we meet after school somewhere or maybe I can get a reprieve, and we can meet here tomorrow afternoon?"

"We can't," Lori said quickly answering for both of them.

Bone thought it a little strange how fast she turned down the idea.

"Time to go," a voice said from across the room.

He recognized it as belonging to Jake Demos. The owner was masked in the shadow of a pillar in the middle of the room. "Club's closed."

"I guess we better get going," Bone said.

"I have to go to the girl's room," Ashley replied.

"Me, too," Lori said. "You go ahead and go home, Bone.

"I'll wait for you."

"We're closed," Demos said, from the shadows. "Time to go, Bone."

"Okay. I'll wait for you guys outside."

The girls smiled and started walking toward the restrooms. Bone walked to the door and stepped out onto the stairs. He took a few steps and the knuckles on his right hand started to throb. He held them up and touched them with his other hand. They hurt. He took another step and suddenly felt dizzy. He stopped and waited until the dizziness went away. He walked through the main room of the club and went out the front door.

The night air was cool and damp. Bone took a deep breath and rubbed his aching knuckles. He looked toward the door expecting to see the girls come out at any moment, but no one appeared. None of the other kids from the room came out the door. No one.

Bone waited.

No one came through the door.

He glanced at his watch. One-fifteen. He looked back at the doorway.

No one exited.

He walked over to the spot where he'd hidden his knapsack and got it out of its hiding place. He started putting on the skates while keeping an eye on the door to the Nightmare Club. Still there was no sign of any of the people from the room. He skated over to the front door of the club to wait for the girls. He wanted to get their phone numbers so they could keep in touch.

The cool air chilled him so Bone decided to wait inside. He reached for the door and pulled. It was locked. Between the crack of the door and the jamb, Bone could see the locked deadbolt.

Thinking it odd, he decided that there had to be another exit to the club about which he didn't know. In his skates, he clumped through the grass to the back of the building and saw a door. He clumsily walked over and checked it. It, too, was locked. He glanced at his watch. One-thirty.

"Man," a frustrated Bone said. "I gotta go."

He clumped through the grass again and made it to the road. He looked back at the building. It looked like an empty hulk. Bone tried to figure out how the girls or anyone for that matter could have left without him seeing them, but he could come up with no answer.

When Bone arrived at his house, he was suddenly confronted with the fact that he had no way to sneak in other than through the front door. Some sneaky method, he thought glumly. But he had no other choice. Bone slipped out of the roller blades and replaced the shoes in the knapsack with the skates. He slipped on the shoes and went to the door. As quietly as he could, he inserted his key into the lock and turned. To Bone, the popping of the lock sounded like a shotgun blast. He froze expecting to hear his dad's footsteps coming down the stairs. But he heard no sound from inside the house. He grabbed the door knob and turned. The door opened. He had never noticed that it creaked until that moment. He winced at the sound, opened the door, and then shut it as quietly as he could. He turned around and walked past the living room. There sitting in the changing glow of the television sat his father. His heart jumped. He was nabbed!

No, wait a minute! His eyes are closed! He's asleep. A wave of relief swept over Bone.

Slowly, silently, he made his way over to the stairs then rubbed his hand across his face in frustration. He looked back and realized that he hadn't locked the front door. He crept back and turned the lock. It popped. He heard someone call from the living room. He froze and waited for his dad to come around the corner and catch him in the act. His heart thumped hard against his ribs as the tension mounted. Gathering his courage, Bone crept to the corner of the living room entrance and peered around it. He saw his dad staring at him.

"What's wrong?" his dad said, still groggy from being awakened.

"Oh, uh, nothing, I just came down to get a drink." Bone said, making sure that his dad only saw his head. If he saw that his son was fully dressed, Bone would be finished.

"Oh, okay," his dad said, as he looked at the movie on the screen.

Thinking quickly, Bone undressed as fast as he

could and hid his clothes in the hall closet beside the front door. In his underwear, he walked past the living room where his dad had started watching television again.

"Coming to bed, Dad?"

"Yeah, I guess I should." Bone's dad got up and turned off the television. He followed his son up the stairs.

Bone made it to his room and was safe. He saw the shape in his bed and smiled. It really did look like someone was there. His plan had worked to perfection. Bone decided to go straight to bed. He wanted to brush his teeth, but with his dad prowling around, it might draw suspicion if he were to brush his teeth again so he would wait until morning. He went over to the bed, pulled back the covers, and tossed the quilt to the floor. He climbed into bed and closed his eyes. In moments, he was asleep.

Three

At around nine o'clock the next morning, Bone awakened to the sound of his father singing to the Karaoke machine he had bought. His father had a little recording studio in his upstairs den and always sang on Sunday mornings. Normally Bone was awake before these singing sessions began, but because of last night's late night revelry, he had stayed in bed longer than usual.

Bone rubbed the sleep out of his eyes and crawled from his bed. He noticed that a couple of his knuckles were a little swollen, but the dull pain was minor. He recalled the fight with Bull and couldn't believe that it had really happened. If it weren't for his aching knuckles, he would've believed that he had imagined it.

He went downstairs to the kitchen where his mother was preparing breakfast.

"Well, good morning, Harold. You must be well rested after all the sleep you got last night."

Bone stifled a yawn. "Yeah, I was real tired."

A look of concern crossed his mother's face. "Oh, what did you do to your knuckles? They look swollen."

"Oh, uh, I was playing around and hit them against the door jamb."

"Let me see."

"They're okay, Mom."

"Let your mother see them."

Bone clucked his tongue. "Okay." He held his hand out while his mother looked at it.

"Is it sore?"

"A little."

"Can you move your fingers?"

Bone moved his fingers wincing a little at the pain.

"Well, I don't think they were broken. How did you do it again?"

"I told you, I was playing around."

"Doing what?"

"Okay," Bone said acting mad, "I got in a fight with the star fullback at Cooper High and beat him up really bad. I hurt my knuckles on his hard head."

Bone's mom laughed. "Boy, it must be something really dumb if you have to make up a story like that."

"That is exactly what happened."

"*You* got in a fight with the star fullback?" His mother said with a bemused smile on her face that doubted his veracity.

"Okay, I'll tell you the whole story. Last night, I tied an extension cord to the foot of the bed so I could lower myself out the window. When I started down, the knot came undone, and I fell to the ground."

His mother giggled.

Bone continued, "Then I put on my roller blades and skated to the Night Owl Club so I could meet the pretty girl I met the night before and Merritt came in and . . ."

71

Bone's mom laughed and held up her hand for Bone to stop. The amused expression on her face and her shaking head clued Bone as to what his mom thought of his story. "I don't need to hear anymore. You hurt your hand playing."

Bone smiled. Sometimes the truth worked.

After breakfast, Bone started to go outside to get the extension cord he had hidden. His dad stopped him.

"Where are you going?"

"Oh, I forgot," Bone smiled.

"Yeah."

His dad went into the living room to watch the television.

Bone slunk to the hall closet to retrieve his clothes, went up to his room, and thought about last night's adventure. As he considered the events of the evening, he began to wonder how the kids had left the club without him seeing them leave. After closing, he had been outside the whole time. Of course, they could've left when he went around back to see if there was another exit, but there didn't seem to be enough time. The only logical explanation is that they stayed inside the club and left after he did. Maybe for some reason Jake Demos let them stay later. After all they had stayed until 2:30 on Friday night so maybe they had a deal with Demos. Still the whole thing was pretty strange.

In fact, there was something strange about the kids that hung out at the room, but he couldn't put his finger on it. They all seemed to know him and yet he didn't know any of them. He liked Ashley, but he ready acceptance of a potential rival in Lori, was kind of weird. He had to admit that while he had enjoyed the attention last night, now that he thought about it, the situation with the two girls was pretty bizarre.

For a moment, Bone closed his eyes and pictured the girls in his mind. The three of them were at the club. Bone was telling jokes and the girls were laughing loudly. But they didn't seem to be laughing at his jokes. They seemed to be laughing at *him*. The giggles were derisive.

The phone rang beside the bed causing Bone to open his eyes and jump.

He picked up the handset and said, "Hello."

"Is Mr. Grimaldi there?"

"Hey, man, what's up?"

"Nothing," Tony said. "How's prison life?"

"It's an easy gig. Matter of fact, last night I made the great escape."

"You did?"

"Yeah, man, I went to the club to meet Ashley."

"You back on that?"

"It's the truth."

"Are you for real?" Tony said, starting to believe that maybe his friend was telling the truth.

"Yeah, I'm not kidding."

"So you really met this chick at the club?"

"Swear to God."

Tony smiled for his friend. "Well, what happened?"

"Before I tell you, I want you to know I am telling you the absolute truth."

"I said I believed you."

"Yeah, but will you believe it when I tell you that I got in a fight with Bull Merritt and beat his tail?"

"What?"

73

"I swear to God," Bone said, then explained the circumstances of the fight.

"You swear that really happened."

"I've got the sore knuckles to prove it."

"That's unreal."

"Tony, man, I don't know what happened. He pushed me and I just kinda snapped. I hit him right in the nose. It felt awesome."

"I don't doubt it," Tony said, then added in a staged fatherly voice, "I'm proud of you, boy."

"I just hope it's over with him."

"If you whipped him like that, it probably is."

"I hope."

"So, did Ashley see the battle?"

"Yeah, she kinda added fuel to the fire by calling Merritt a jerk."

"Which he is."

"Yeah. So anyway she kissed me after it was over."

"Whoah, Joe Studd, the conquering hero."

Bone smiled. "Now for improbable story number two."

"What's that?"

"Well, this other girl, Lori, came up to me after the fight and I ended up dancing with her and Ashley all night. I didn't get home until one."

Tony shook his head. "Aw, man, you're making this hard for me to believe."

"Even the infamous Bone man wouldn't make up this one."

"That's true," Tony agreed. "So did you get two phone numbers or what?"

"Or what."

"What do you mean?"

74

"Well, at one o'clock, Demos came into the room and told everybody they were closing."

"I thought the club closed at midnight."

"So did I, but maybe this room stays open later or something. So anyway, he told us to leave so I went outside to wait for the girls 'cause they went to the bathroom. Anyway, they never showed. They didn't come out."

"Maybe they went out the back."

"Yeah, but I told them I was waiting for them. I even checked out back and the door was locked."

"You got me," Tony said, puzzled by the scenario.

"I guess Demos must've let them stay. It's the only explanation."

"Maybe they slipped him some cash. Are they from the riding academy? Those chicks have bucks."

"No, I don't think so. I really don't know where they're from. They don't talk about themselves much. I'm their favorite subject."

"Get out the shovels, it's getting deep," Tony said.

Bone laughed, but what he said was true.

"So, you still on restriction?" Tony asked.

"Yeah. But maybe you can come over and we can shoot some hoops or play Goblins on the Nintendo. I'll ask my dad and call you back."

"Okay, and I'll ask Aunt Ann."

"Cool. Call you back in a minute."

"Later."

Bone hung up the phone. It felt great to tell someone about the fight with Merritt. He couldn't tell his dad about the scrap without revealing his breach of curfew.

He started to get up to go ask his dad if Tony could

75

come over when the door opened to his room.

"Harold, what happened to your bike?" Dad said, coming into the room.

Bone thought quickly. "Oh, uh, I crashed it. I wasn't paying attention and hit a fire hydrant. I, uh, hurt my hand, too, see?"

He held up the damaged knuckles so that his dad could see. He knew his dad would tell his mom about the "accident" and that would complete the story for her.

"Well, your mom and I are going over to the grocery store. You want us to stop and drop off your tire to get it fixed at the Bike Shoppe?"

"Are they open on Sunday?"

"I think so."

"Okay, that'd be great."

"Be more careful when you're riding the bike. Next time, the repairs come out of your pocket."

"Thanks, Dad. Oh, Dad, I know I'm on restriction, but could Tony come over for a little bit and play some hoops?"

Bone's dad pursed his lips. "I guess so. Tony's a good kid. How's his aunt doing, anyway?"

"Not too good."

"That's a shame. She is a nice lady."

"Yeah."

His dad shook his head. "Well, I better get going. You guys stay around the house."

"We will."

His dad nodded and left.

Bone picked up the phone and dialed his friend's number.

Tony answered.

"You can come over," Bone said.

"Cool, but I can only stay a couple of hours."

"Okay."

"See ya in a bit."

"Later."

Ten minutes later, the doorbell rang. Bone hustled down the stairs and opened the front door. It was Tony.

"Hey, Joe Studd," Tony said.

"Cool it, man, or I'll punch you out," Bone said. Tony acted scared.

Bone laughed. "Come on in, dude."

"Where's the folks?"

"Out shopping."

"What do you want to get whipped at first, hoops or Nintendo?"

"You can *try* to whip me in hoops."

"Let's go."

The two teens went outside. Bone got the basketball out of the garage and popped a shot at the basket and backboard set up over the garage. He missed the rim completely.

"Air ball," Tony said, picking up the ball and swishing it through the hoop. "Nothing but net," Tony exclaimed.

"Lucky shot," Bone said, slapping the ball out of Tony's hands. He grabbed it, shot, and missed by a foot.

Tony laughed and retrieved the ball. "Hey, I asked Pam about Cindy and Kevin last night." He shot and made another basket.

"Oh, yeah, why bother? Cindy and Kevin were pretty tight on the dance floor," Bone said as he caught the ball and threw it to his friend for another shot.

"They were just dancing."

"So what did she say about them?" Bone asked.

"You're not really interested, are you? I mean a guy that's got two girls —"

In principle, Bone agreed with Tony that he shouldn't be interested, but he was. Although Ashley and Lori were both foxes, they were kind of strange, whereas Cindy was not as pretty, but was normal. Besides he was on a roll and who says a guy can't have three girlfriends. "Come on, man, what'd she say?"

Tony threw up a shot and missed. Bone grabbed the rebound and put it up. "She said Cindy wasn't serious about Kevin."

"Really?"

"Man, you sure are anxious for a guy who danced with two girls last night."

"I wouldn't mind giving Cindy a shot at me, too," Bone said arrogantly.

"Oh, you wouldn't," Tony laughed, surprised by his friend's newfound confidence. He wondered if it was for real. "So, ask her out."

"I might just do that," Bone said, confidently, but the statement made his stomach tighten. It seemed so easy to ask Ashley and Lori to dance or meet him in the room at the Night Owl Club, but the thought of asking Cindy Macleod out made him nervous. Where was his newly discovered poise?

"If you want, I'll get her phone number from Pam tomorrow at school," Tony said, making another basket. "I'm gonna burn you today, home boy."

"Just wait on getting the number. I might ask her

face to face."

"Oh, right," Tony said. Was Bone starting to wimp out on him?

"Man, just let me do it my way."

"Chill. I will," Tony said, then tossed the ball to his friend. "Now let's play some ball. Take it out."

Bone dribbled onto the driveway and the game was on.

After the game which Bone lost 21-4, Bone and Tony went into the kitchen and got a drink of iced tea. They both drank two big glasses and then went up to Bone's room and played a couple of games of Goblins.

"I gotta go," Tony said when he looked at the clock on the dresser. He got up and handed Bone the controller to the video system.

"Okay, I'll see you."

"You sure you don't want me to get Pam to give me that phone number?"

"Yeah, I'm sure."

"Okay. I'll see you at the school tomorrow."

"Later. Hey, lock the door on your way out."

Tony nodded and left the room.

Bone was playing the game again when he heard the doorbell ring a few minutes later.

"Dummy locked the door and forgot something," Bone said, as he hurried out of the room and down the stairs.

He unlocked the door and opened it.

"What'd you forget . . . ?" Bone said, as a fist collided with his cheek. Stars flashed as he went down to one knee. He looked up and saw two black eyes underlined by white bandages across a broken nose.

Bone stood up as Bull Merritt threw another punch. Bone ducked the blow and came across with one of his own. The skinny kid hit the football star in the face, but the punch had no effect. In fact, it did nothing but send a jolt of pain up Bone's arm. Bull smiled and hit Bone square in the chest. His sternum lit up with agony.

"Nobody whips me," Bull growled as he grabbed Bone and threw him outside. Bone landed in the grass and scrambled to his feet. He put up his fists and could feel the rage returning as he tasted blood inside his mouth. Bone attacked, Bull stood his ground and punched him in the face. The thin kid went down hard. Bull jumped on top of him and ground his face into the yard.

"You got lucky last night," Bull said, viciously grinding Bone's face into the grass as he slapped his ears.

Bone couldn't get Bull off him as Merritt continued the assault. He started crying in frustration and pain. Merritt laughed and stood up. Bone got to his feet and started to run.

Merritt just watched him and laughed.

"Go on, chicken. Run. We're even now."

Bull saw the Fenimores' car coming up the road and took off. Running to his Mustang, he jumped in it and sped away, tires squealing.

Bone saw him leave and stopped running. He was gasping and trembling. What had happened? Last night he was a tiger and today he was a kitten. He tried to catch his breath. The air smelled like exhaust fumes and grass, and he remembered the sweet air of the room. Oh, how he craved it. It made him feel good. It reminded him of his victory.

He saw his parents pull into the driveway, and he ran to hide. But a thought stopped him in his tracks; if he hid, they would think that he had gone somewhere and broken his restriction. Reluctantly, he went into the house and ran up to the bathroom. He washed the dirt and blood off his face and checked the damage. He had a cut on the inside of his mouth and his cheek was swollen, but not badly. Maybe he could keep the fight from his parents. He knew if he told them about Bull's attack, they would call Merritt's folks and the fullback would probably get in trouble and then the whole thing would start over again. Better to keep quiet. He went into his room to change clothes.

"Bone, you here?"

"Up in my room playing Nintendo," Bone said as he turned on the game. He heard footsteps coming up the stairs.

"Who was that in the Mustang?" his dad said, as he came into the room.

"Oh, uh, that was Alvin Merritt."

"Alvin Merritt? I don't think I've met him."

"He just came by to play ball," Bone kept his swollen jaw away from his father's point of view.

"I thought Tony was coming over?"

"He did, but he had to go home. So me and Alvin played, but I, uh, caught an elbow and we quit. See?" He turned to show his dad his cheek.

"You better put some ice on that," Bone's dad said. "Take down the swelling."

"I guess."

"Try not to let your mom see it, you know how she

81

gets."

"I'll try."

"You're getting pretty banged up this week. First the knuckles and then your cheek."

"Yeah, I guess I need to start wearing body armor."

Dad smiled. "Well, come on down to the kitchen and get something on it," he said as he started out the room. Bone turned off the game and followed him downstairs to get some ice.

While his dad went into the living room, Bone went into the kitchen. He found a bag of frozen peas in the freezer and put them against his jaw. The cold felt good at first, but then began to hurt.

He went back up to his room, holding the bag against his cheek. When he got inside his room, he went over and dropped onto his bed. The left side of his face throbbed. In one night and one day, he had gone from hero to loser. He had hoped that last night's beating would've made Bull think twice about fighting him, but apparently he had been wrong about the fullback. Merritt's thirst for revenge was greater than the damage Bone had inflicted. The mind set of those kind of guys was baffling to Bone. But what puzzled him even more was how Merritt had handled him. Last night, it had been so easy to beat the big kid. But today Bone's blows had been totally worthless. He could've been hitting Bull with a feather for all the damage he caused. He couldn't figure it out, and the headache that was building in his skull didn't help.

After another fifteen minutes of pressing the bag of frozen peas to his cheek, Bone checked himself in the mirror and saw that the swelling had gone down to almost normal. He went downstairs and returned the bag of peas to the freezer. Then he went into the living room where his dad was reclining on the couch looking through the paper and his mom was reading a book. Bone turned on the television, flipped the station to an old horror movie and settled in to watch.

An hour later, his eyelids drooped and sleep took him.

While he slept, Bone dreamed of the room at the club. He could smell the sweet aroma of the mist. The glass globe spun webs of light that trapped him in their beauty. He saw Ashley and Lori waving to him. He tried to get to them, but was held back by something. He struggled against the unseen force which gripped him. The girls smiled and beckoned him to join them, but he couldn't move.

"Let me go," Bone said, then turned to face the thing that held him.

A punch thumped against his head. He saw stars.

Ashley and Lori laughed.

Another punch collided with his cheek.

Bone could hear the laughter of the girl and that of his tormentor, Bull Merritt.

"Dipwad," Merritt said, as he drove his fist into Bone's ribs.

Bone took a deep breath trying to get some air. The mist in the room filled his lungs. Suddenly, he felt strong. He broke away from Merritt's clutches and turned around to face him. Bone threw a punch, hitting Merritt in the forehead.

"What the heh —" Bone's dad's voice came out of Merritt's mouth. "Harold!"

Bone jumped and opened his eyes. His dad was

staring at him.

"What are you doing?" Bone's dad said.

"Huh?" a confused Bone replied.

"You punched the coffee table and scared the crap out of me."

"Sorry. I was dreaming I guess."

"Well, okay," Dad said, calming down.

Bone sat up on the couch and wiped the sweat off his forehead. The rest of Sunday passed without any more trouble.

Four

Monday morning Bone was back in school. When he went to his locker to get his books for first and second period, Tony was there waiting for him.

"What happened to you?" he said, noticing the bruise on his cheek.

"Bull Merritt jumped me after you left yesterday."

"What?"

"I went to the door and he hit me before I had a chance."

"That's bogus," Tony said angrily.

"Chill, Tone, man, it's over for now. I don't wait to start anything else."

Just then as if by fate, Bull Merritt and Truck Calhoun came around the corner. Tony's mouth dropped open when he saw the condition of Merritt's face. Both eyes were black and his nose was bandaged. He looked like a one armed prizefighter after a championship fight.

Merritt looked over at Bone and smiled. Bone looked away. Tony glared at the football star, but said nothing.

Bull and Truck glanced at Bone and laughed, but kept going. The feud was over as far as they were concerned.

"Man, you really did do a number on his face," Tony said. Up until then, he thought that maybe Bone had gotten in a lucky shot and then the fight was broken up. He figured Bone merely exaggerated the fight, but Merritt's face indicated a much more severe beating.

"Yeah, and then yesterday I couldn't do squat. I hit him in the face, and he laughed."

"Just be glad he didn't do to your face what you did to his face."

Bone smiled, causing a twinge of pain in his jaw.

The bell rang.

"Gotta go," Tony said.

"I'll see you next period."

"Cool."

As Bone walked down the hallway, he recognized Cindy Macleod's pretty blonde hair as she walked across the main courtyard of the campus. His heart tripped. She looked his way and waved. He waved back and she slowed down to talk. Bone walked over to her.

"Hey, Cindy," he said.

"Hi."

"So what's up?"

"Have you seen your friend, Bull, today?"

"Yeah."

"Somebody told me that he got jumped by some academy guys Saturday night."

"What?"

"That's what Bull told them."

"He's lying. We got in a fight."

Cindy chuffed a laugh. "Oh, Bone, you are so funny."

"No, really. At the club."

Cindy giggled. "You crack me up. You beating Bull

86

Merritt like that. *Not!*"

Bone smiled, knowing that he could never convince her. "Well, I didn't tell you. I changed into Mr. Hyde first. See I took this special drug and changed into a monster."

Cindy smiled and rolled her eyes. "You're something. You know that?"

"Yeah, but what?"

Cindy laughed and started to walk toward class.

"See ya," Bone said.

"Bye," Cindy said, then giggled one last time.

As Bone watched her walk away, he decided that today would be the day. Today he was going to ask her out. After last period, he would do it.

The bell rang loudly, ending the day of classes. Bone watched Cindy get up from her seat and gather her books. His stomach rumbled as he tried to gather his courage. He got up and put his books in his knapsack. Cindy was starting out the door. Bone watched her and decided to let her go. He would ask her tomorrow.

No! a voice in his head shouted. Ask her now. The other girls liked you and they didn't even know you. Ask her.

Bone hurried out of the room and saw Cindy walking down the hallway toward the bus stop.

"Hey, Cindy," Bone called out.

She turned and saw him waving. She stopped.

A swarm of bees seemed to be buzzing inside Bone's stomach as he walked toward the girl.

"Hey, Bone. What's up?"

"I, uh, I wanted to talk to you."

"About what?"

"Well, I was thinking that maybe, well . . ."

"What, Bone?"

"Would you want to, uh, go out to dinner or something with me?"

Cindy laughed. "Go out to dinner with you? What's the joke?"

"Huh?" Bone said, confused by her laughter.

"The joke? What are you gonna do to me?"

"Do? Nothing, I just thought we could go out to dinner or something."

"Oh, sure. And then you show up dressed like a geek or something and you guys videotape it. No thanks."

"No, really. I want to go out with you."

Cindy shook her head. "I know you, Bone. No thanks."

Bone was taken aback. He hadn't expected his reputation as a joker to get in the way. It was obvious that Cindy didn't believe that he really wanted to go out with her. "Cindy, I'm not gonna play any tricks."

"Oh sure. Listen, Bone, I have to catch the bus."

"But I really—"

"You're not gonna get me to fall for it, okay? Now—"

"I know. You have to catch the bus," Bone said, dejectedly. "I'll see you."

"Okay. Nice try, Bone," Cindy said, giggling.

"Bye," Bone said, as he watched her walk away from him. His face felt flush and his stomach was tied in knots. His shirt clung to his sweaty back. The pain of Cindy's rejection cut deeply into his spirit. He knew he shouldn't have asked her. How could he have thought that a girl like Cindy would want to go out with a dweeb like him? His eyes began to fill with tears. He swiped at them angrily with his forearm.

Just then a familiar scent of perfume drifted past him. He turned expecting to see Ashley standing next to him.

No one was there.

He sniffed the air and caught the scent again. He recognized it and knew why it reminded him of Ashley. It was the same sweet smell as the mist at the club. He breathed it in and started to feel better. Slowly his feelings of rejection began to burn away in a wave of anger.

Who was Cindy Macleod to snub him like that? She was just using his reputation as a joker as an excuse to turn him down. He thought about the girls at the club. They liked his sense of humor and were twice as pretty as stupid Cindy. If she thought she was too cool to go out with him then he would just have to let the two girls at the club have him all for themselves. Bone pictured the club with its spinning lights and all the good-looking people and how they treated him like the big man on campus. He could see Ashley and Lori's pretty faces. Sure it was a little strange the way they shared him. And the fact that they knew him before he had ever laid eyes on either of them was certainly on the odd side, but they thought he was great so what did it matter? Cindy's rejection made him want to see them to reaffirm that he was wanted by some people. He had to go to the club that night to see his real friends.

Immediately a plan of deception came to him. He would tell his parents he was going over to Tony's to study and then go to the club for a little while. He would stay until around nine-thirty, then return home. If he played his cards right, his parents would be none the wiser.

With the vague scent of the mist lingering in his mind, he started for the bike racks in the parking lot.

"Oh, no," Bone said, "I have detention today." He turned around and started running for the cafeteria. Being late to detention was an automatic extra day and Coach Yarborough, the gym teacher was a stickler for rules. As he ran he looked at his watch, he had one minute to get all the way across campus. He picked up the pace.

"Hey, Bone!" Tony called out when he saw his running friend. He and Pam were talking at the lockers.

"Can't stop. Got detention!" Bone shouted as a book bounced out of his knapsack and landed behind him. "Shoot," the teen hissed as he stopped to pick up the book.

"Nice trick!" Tony shouted as he and Pam laughed.

"Funny, Tone," Bone said as he put the book back into the knapsack and then took off running.

When Bone got to the cafeteria, he reached for the doors and pulled. They clanked and didn't open. He was late. He looked through the window and saw the coach coming slowly toward the door. He was smiling. The coach pushed open the door.

"Come on in, Fenimore," he said. "You get another day."

Bone smiled halfheartedly and went to take his seat. As he took out his history book to study, his mind wandered back to the club.

"So can I go?" Bone said as he scooped a spoonful of peas into his mouth.

"If you guys are really going to study you can go," Bone's mom said. "I know how you get when you start

90

playing that video game."

"Tony's machine's busted. We really are going to study."

"Okay, but how are you going to get there?"

"I was hoping I could borrow the car."

"Harv?"

With a mouthful of food, Bone's dad nodded then swallowed, "Just make sure you don't race the engine."

"I won't," Bone said, rolling his eyes. His dad's car was a Yugo and revving the engine was hardly an exciting event.

"Okay."

"I want you back here by nine."

"We have a lot of stuff to go over. Can I make it ten?"

"Nine-thirty."

"Okay," Bone said, playing his parents like a fiddle. Nine-thirty was the time he wanted to get home anyway.

He finished his dinner and went up to his room to get ready.

Bone didn't expect the Night Owl Club to be crowded and he was right. A few guys from the Hudson Academy were playing pool. Couples dotted a few tables in the main room sharing burgers and fries, but otherwise it was pretty dead.

"Hey, Jenny," Bone said, as he passed the blonde. "How's it going?"

"Oh, hey, it's the Bud light Man."

Bone smiled. "Yeah."

"It's about an average Monday night."

"Where's your dad? I see he's not behind the snack bar."

"No. He, uh, stepped out for a little while."

A girl motioned toward Jenny.

"Got a customer. See you."

"Right," Bone said as he made his way to the back of the club.

When he stepped into the storeroom area where the door to the stairwell was located, Bone got that same creepy feeling he'd felt that first night he'd found the door. There was something about the silence of the room that was chilling. It just seemed to be a place where no one ventured. He shuddered and walked through the room, stopping at the door to the stairwell. Bone opened it and stepped onto the platform. He went down the stairs and opened the door to the room. He stood there for a moment dumbstruck. The room was filled with teenagers. It looked like it was a Friday or Saturday night. The music blared. Kids danced.

"I thought you weren't coming," a voice whispered in Bone's ear, startling him. He turned and saw Ashley standing beside him.

"Oh, hey, Ashley, I decided to come and see what was up."

Ashley smiled. "Come on over to the table."

Bone followed Ashley to their usual table. Lori was there as well as Bob and Jackie.

They exchanged greetings.

Bone saw someone sitting in a darkened corner of the room. It looked like an adult. He just sat there watching the kids. Bone figured it was Jake Demos.

"So what's happening?" Bone said.

"We heard you had a little trouble with that jerk that came in here Saturday night. The one you beat up," Lori said.

"Who told you that?" Bone said. The only person he had told about Merritt's sneak attack was Tony.

"A friend at school," she said.

"What friend?"

"A friend of your friend." Lori grinned coyly.

Bone couldn't believe that Tony had told anyone about the fight especially when he had told him to drop it. "Are you saying Tony told a friend of yours about the fight?"

Ashley smiled. "Let's dance, Bone."

"Wait a sec."

"Come on, let's dance. Lori's just playing with you."

Bone started to continue, but Ashley took his hand and led him to the floor. They started to dance.

As Bone breathed in the sweet mist, he felt better. When he thought about it, he didn't really care if Tony told anyone about the fight. He would whip Bull's butt again if he ever showed his face around here. In fact, he *wanted* Bull to show up at the club. He wanted revenge for the ambush of yesterday.

After a while, Lori came out to the dance floor. "Cutting in," she said as she stood next to the couple. Ashley smiled and let her.

At first, Bone felt weird again about the girls sharing him, but he quickly forgot about it as Lori nuzzled her lips into his neck. He shivered with delight.

Lori smiled. "I just called Bull Merritt and told him to come over—since that's what you wanted."

"What?" Bone said, suddenly confused. He hadn't told Lori that he wanted Merritt to show up. It had just been a thought!

"I told him you wanted to see him here at the club," the pretty red-head repeated.

93

Bone was about to protest but stopped. He really did want Bull to come to the room. He remembered the ambush and how Bull had rubbed his face in the ground. How he had laughed and taunted him. Bone's face began to flush with anger. He clenched his jaw. Let him come, he thought grimly, just let him show that ugly face in here. I'll finish this thing once and for all.

"I have something to help you end it," Lori said.

Bone didn't notice that she seemed to have read his mind.

The grin on Lori's face made her look like a hungry tigress. She took Bone's hand and led him over to the table. They sat down and she pulled a knife from her purse.

"Take this," she said.

Bone picked up the knife and pressed the switch. It clicked open and the shiny blade caught a shaft of light. Bone grinned, pushed it shut, and then flicked it open again. He took a breath and felt the bravado of justifed anger course through his blood.

"Let him come," Bone said, eyeing the door to the room.

The teenagers sitting around the table grinned. A shadowy figure in the corner of the room shifted in his seat in anticipation of the confrontation.

Five minutes passed.

Bone flicked the knife open and then closed it. A strange smile twisted his features. He looked demonic.

Ten minutes.

The clicking of the knife as it opened and closed sounded like a clock. A ticking time bomb that would strike Bull Merritt very soon.

Fifteen minutes.

Bone stared at the door. Waiting. Breathing steadily. The malevolent grin was still carved in his face.

Twenty minutes passed.

The door opened and Bull Merritt stepped inside the room. He scanned the crowd until his eyes fell on Bone Fenimore.

"You dipwad, you didn't get enough," he shouted then took a step toward his enemy. He stopped suddenly and took a step backward. Then another, his mouth opening in awestruck fear. The kids in the room! They were . . . they were . . . No. No. It couldn't be, thought Bull.

"What's wrong, Bull?" Jackie Pressman said as a maggot dripped out of his ear. He was suddenly standing beside Merritt.

Bull turned and held back a shriek when he saw Jackie's decayed face.

Bone smiled when he saw Merritt and clicked open the knife Lori had given him. He got up from the table and started for the frightened kid.

Merritt turned and started to run for the door. A moldering corpse of a girl shambled into his path and tripped him. He fell, but quickly scrambled to his feet.

Bone stopped for a moment when he saw the scared expression on Merritt's face. He looked down at the knife in his hand and stared at it as if it were something alien. A scream snapped his attention back to Bull Merritt.

The fullback was running wildly for the door having seen one of Jackie's eyes fall out of its socket. His face was white as a sheet.

Bone heard the kids in the room laugh at the panicked Bull. But their laughter had an odd ring to it.

Something about the sound of it was just a little off kilter. Bone didn't pause long to think about it. Taking a breath, he smiled cruelly then started running toward Bull.

In a state of panic, Merritt grabbed the door knob, twisted it, and threw open the door. Bone was right behind him. He came down with the knife. It narrowly missed the fleeing fullback, stabbing the rail of the stairwell instead. Bone extracted the blade and started after Merritt. He took a couple of steps toward Bull. Puffing from his exertions, Bone staggered to a stop. The world seemed to rotate under his feet, and he wavered. Glancing up, he saw Bull climbing on all fours to the top of the steps. The guy was blubbering incoherently as he opened the door and scrambled out of sight.

Sitting down heavily on the steps, Bone looked at the knife in his hand. What was he doing with it? He didn't remember having a knife when he came into the club. He looked back at the door to the room and was surprised to see that none of the partyers had followed him out. Staggering to his feet, he walked back to the door. Then he looked in, and for a moment, he was startled. The room was different. It was old and decaying. He rubbed his eyes and looked again. Now the room was bright and new. He saw Ashley and the others sitting at the table where he'd left them. He looked once more at the knife in his hand—but saw that he had been somehow mistaken. It was nothing but a pen. He laughed at that. Tossing it away, he stepped back into the room to join the others.

For the rest of the night Bone danced with both girls. Occasionally, he went back to the table to treat Jackie and Bob to a series of jokes and funny stories. Once it seemed like the entire room had gathered around him as he got on one of his fabled rolls and had everyone cracking up with laughter. Bone had never felt so important.

At ten o'clock, Bone realized that he was late for home.

"Well, I'm late again," Bone said. "I guess I better go."

"Why don't you stay a little longer?" Ashley said, "After all, you're already in trouble so why not stay and have fun?"

"I'm not that late. Only a half hour. Right now, I might just get yelled at. If I stay any later, I'll be back on restriction for sure."

Ashley looked disappointed. "Just a little while. Till ten-thirty."

"Really, Ash, I have to go."

"Can't you call your dad and tell him you're having car trouble," Lori said, adding her two cents.

"Then he'll get all freaked out. I'm just gonna go."

"Fine," Ashley said, starting to pout.

"Come on, don't be that way. I really have to go."

"So go."

Bone got up and started for the door. He looked back and saw Ashley staring at him. When their eyes met, she looked away from him. Bone took a deep breath and sighed. He started back for the table.

"Well, maybe for another half hour," Bone said, smiling. "I can always play secret agent and sneak out if I get restricted."

An hour later, Bone said goodbye to his friends. He knew his butt was burned, but he didn't care. He was the king of the room and these were his subjects.

On the ride home, Bone recalled the incident with Bull. It seemed to have happened a long time ago — if it had happened at all. Maybe he had just imagined that the fullback had come to the Night Owl Club. He tried to remember the specifics, but his memory was blurred. Did Bull have a knife? Or did I have it? Bone rubbed his eyes with the palm of his hands. Did we fight? He didn't feel sore anywhere, so he doubted it.

A car's horn blared, startling him. Bone snapped to attention and swerved out of the way of a car backing out of the driveway. He realized that he had been driving on the wrong side of the street.

Steering back onto the proper side of the road, Bone shook his head to clear the cobwebs. Suddenly, he realized that he was in front of his house. He applied the brakes, turned the small car into the driveway, and parked.

When he got inside the house, his dad was waiting for him. Harv immediately started shouting, "What the hell has gotten into you lately? You are an hour and a half late. I called over to Tony's house at ten and woke everyone up. They said you had never been there. Where the hell were you?"

"I, uh, I was at the Night Owl Club," Bone said, deciding to tell the truth and take the consequences.

"On a school night?" His dad asked, sounding unconvinced.

"Yes, sir, I had a date with a girl."

"I don't care if you had a date with Princess Diana. You lied to me and your mother."

"I know. But you wouldn't have let me go if I had told you the truth."

"Oh, so you lie to us to get your way. Great." His

dad's face got red. "Get your butt up to your room and get used to it. You'll be spending the rest of the week there."

"Yes, sir." Bone said, knowing that nothing he said at this point would make a difference. If only he hadn't let Ashley's pouting act get to him. Then he would've only been a half hour late and just gotten a good scolding. His dad wouldn't have called Tony's and found out that he wasn't there. His whole plan fell apart because of the manipulations of that girl. Oh well, he thought, get used to it. Such is the way of the world. Bone smiled at his sexist remark.

"Something funny?" Bone's dad growled.

"Huh," Bone said, unaware of his smiling face.

"What the hell are you grinning about?"

"Oh, uh, nothing. Sorry, Dad," Bone replied, wiping the smile off his face.

"Get to bed!"

Bone nodded and ran up the stairs.

Five

Bone's night was far from restful. A frightening nightmare left him with a vague sense of foreboding. He was in the room at the club and all the kids were listening to him as he told a series of jokes. He was on a stage, or maybe it was just a table, but he remembered he was a stand-up comedian. There was even a spotlight on him. He got on a roll and the crowd was roaring. Their laughter swarmed over him like a ticklish hive of bees. He told one of his favorite jokes and the crowd started laughing and applauding. The laughter felt wonderful until the spotlight swung around and he saw the crowd of teenagers. They were giggling and laughing as their faces crumbled to reveal the skulls and withered flesh of animated corpses.

Bone woke up in a sweat at the sight of this audience of cadavers. He glanced at the clock and saw that it was five-thirty. He still had thirty minutes before he had to get up for school. He tried to get back to sleep, but the minute he closed his eyes a decayed face with stringy hair and eyeless sockets would creep into his consciousness and he would open his eyes to chase it away. He stayed in bed until the alarm rang, then got up, and began his day as usual.

After getting dressed, Bone went downstairs to the dining room where his mother was putting breakfast on the table. Bone sat in his chair. His father was already at the table sipping a cup of coffee and reading the newspaper.

"Morning, Mom," Bone said as his mom sat at the table to eat.

"Good morning," his mother said testily. He knew she was mad at him for lying to her and his dad.

"Morning, Dad," Bone said, testing the waters.

"Morning," his dad grunted.

Hmm, Bone thought, I guess a grunt is better than having him start in on me about last night. Something must be pretty interesting in the paper.

Bone buttered a slice of toast.

"What was the name of that kid that was playing basketball with you the other day?" Bone's dad asked, looking up from the paper.

"You mean, Bull Merritt?"

"Maybe. Is his real name Alvin Merritt?"

"Yeah," Bone said as he got a sinking feeling in his stomach. "Why, Dad?"

"The paper says he was found in the woods beside the Night Owl Club last night."

Bone's stomach did a somersault. Hadn't he and Merritt fought? And wasn't there a knife involved? He tried to keep the quiver out of his voice as he asked, "Is he dead?"

"Dead? Oh no. He was just wandering around. The police said that he was totally incoherent. They took him to the mental ward of the hospital for observation."

"Oh, man," Bone said.

"Did you see him when you were there last night?" Dad asked.

"Huh?" Bone said, stunned by the paper's revelation.

"Did you see Alvin Merritt last night after you lied to us and went to the club?"

"Oh, uh, no, no, I didn't," Bone lied.

"Hmm, I wonder what happened to him to make him go crazy," Mom said.

Yeah, Bone thought, I wonder what happened to him, too.

After arriving at school and stopping by his own locker, Bone walked to Tony's locker. He saw Tony getting his books and went over to talk to him.

"Hey, Tone, what's up?"

"Nada."

"Did you read about Bull Merritt in the paper?" Bone asked.

"What'd he do? Score five touchdowns or something?"

"No, man, he went crazy."

"Went crazy — what are you talking about?"

"He went crazy. They found him wandering around in the woods by the Nightmare Club."

"You're lying," Tony said, closing his locker.

"No. I swear. I was there last night."

"At the club?"

"Yeah, I met the girls there and Merritt came into the room and started coming at me, but then he . . ."

Bone stopped as he tried to recall what had happened.

"He what?"

"He left." Bone said, unable to fill in the details.

"Did you guys get into it again?"

"I don't . . . no, we didn't." Bone wasn't sure.

"And they found him in the woods?"

"Yeah, but now he's in the mental ward at the hospital now."

"Mental ward?"

"I told you he went nuts."

"Man, that's weird."

"Yeah, it is."

"I wonder what happened to him?"

"I don't know," Bone said.

The two guys stood at the locker for a moment, both lost in their thoughts.

"I guess since he went nuts he won't be bothering you anymore," Tony said finally.

"I guess not," Bone said. "But I bet he starts having bigtime problems with squirrels."

Tony laughed and shook his head. "Weak, man, very weak."

"So, Pam told me that you asked Cindy out."

Bone's ears reddened.

"What's the deal?" Tony asked.

Bone sighed. "She thought I was setting her up for a practical joke."

"You told her you weren't, right?"

"What do you think I am? A dweeb?"

"Well, yeah," Tony said with a smirk.

"Real funny," Bone said, a little irritated at his friend's comment. Tony had never seen the way the

103

kids in the room at the club treated him. Like he was important—the main man.

"Don't get mad at me because of your rep as the Funny Bone," Tony said, seeing the anger in Bone's eyes.

"Well," Bone said, "I'm glad she didn't say yes or I might not have gone to the room at the club last night. I had a blast."

"Speaking of that, when am I gonna get to meet these girls?"

"Next time I go to the club, I'll call you."

The bell rang for first period to begin. "Deal, man. I better get to class. I'll see you in Spanish," Tony said.

"*Si, si, señor,*" Bone replied.

He walked to his first class, hoping he would see Cindy Macleod. She had history in the room around the corner from his class, and he usually saw her on his way. He made up his mind that if he did see her today, he would snub her like she had snubbed him.

But she must have already gone to class because Bone didn't see her. His plan to ignore her would have to wait.

As he looked around the campus for her one last time, he was suddenly struck by a thought. Why had he never seen his buddies from the club, Jackie Pressman and Bob Wisniski, at school? They had told him that they went to Cooper High and yet, even though he now knew them, he had never seen them at school.

Oh well, they probably have totally different schedules than me, Bone thought. He would ask them about it the next time he saw them in the room at the

Nightmare Club.

He shrugged and went to class.

That afternoon, after serving his time in detention, Bone arrived home and went up to his room — or "cell," as he had taken to calling it. Within ten minutes, he was bored and decided to pass the time playing his newest video game, Troll Trashers.

As Bone played, he began to settle into the rhythm of the game. His man bashed and trashed trolls with a club, then dumped them into the trashcan on his back.

When his man stepped into the final room, Bone stared at the screen and gasped. The room was on the screen . . . *The* room! The room at the club!

His little warrior stepped inside the room on the screen and suddenly Bone felt himself become that warrior. He could feel the club in his hand. He could smell the sweet aroma of the mist. He looked around and saw Ashley and Lori. They were chained to the wall at the far end of the room. Bone took a step forward.

A door opened.

Bone clutched the club.

From behind the door stepped the giant troll. Only it wasn't the giant troll, named Terrible Tiny, it was Bull Merritt dressed in the same clothes as the game troll. A shabby fur bodice covered his muscular torso. His feet and calves were encased in a pair of hairy boots. He wore spiked bracelets on his wrists and a lunatic grin on his face. In his hand, he held the switchblade knife that Lori had given Bone last night.

"Hey, dipwad, I'm gonna cut your head off," Merritt said as he bounded across the room loping like the troll in the game.

Bone tried to move sideways out of the way, but found that he could only move backward and forward just like the warrior in the game.

"Help us, Bone," the girls exclaimed with strangely synthetic voices. "Help us, Bone."

Bone backed away from the charging Bull Troll. He raised the club. He could feel himself pressing the action button on the controller while at the same time bringing the club down on the troll thing's head. He felt both inside and outside of the room on the screen.

The troll backed away and sliced at him with the knife. He moved backward and dodged the slashing thrust. The Bull Troll laughed and lunged again. Bone pressed the jump button and leapt over the oncoming monster. He landed behind him and struck several times with the club. The troll turned slowly and started toward Bone again.

Bone backed away raising the club. He jumped and clubbed at the same time. He hit Bull on top of the head. The troll fell to one knee.

After jumping on top of him, Bone started swinging the club again.

The Troll lashed out with the knife. Bone felt a slash of pain against his ribs. He leapt away, but he was too late to miss another knife thrust into his ribs. Pain ripped through his body. It felt as though the knife had pierced a lung. He took a breath and pain lanced him through the chest. He took another breath

106

and smelled the sweet aroma of the mist. It soothed his pain. He raised the club and brought it down on the troll's head. Bull quivered and fell to his knee again. Bone struck him again with the club. And again.

The troll shook and then fell. Bone jumped over the troll and ran over to the girls.

"Help us, Bone," they said. "We need you."

Bone brought the club down on their chains. The chains wouldn't break. He hit them again. Still they held fast, which meant only one thing . . .

He turned and saw that the Bull Troll was charging. Bone pressed the jump button, but the Troll struck a blow to his leg. He landed and almost fell. He had been hit three times.

All of a sudden, Bone realized that according to the rules of the game, if he was hit two more times with the knife he would *die*. He prepared to fight for his life as the Bull Troll charged him again.

Tony heard a crashing sound come from the living room. He jumped up from the kitchen table where he'd been doing his homework and ran into the living room. He saw his aunt lying across the coffee table. Her glasses askew on her face. Popcorn was all over the floor. She had fallen when she had tried to get up for a drink. Tony rushed to her side.

"Aunt Ann, are you okay?"

His aunt mumbled something unintelligible.

"Aunt Ann?" Tony said, a little bit scared.

He helped her to the couch and laid her down.

"Aunt Ann, should I call the nurse back?" The home health nurse had just left, and Tony was supposed to look after his aunt until the next nurse arrived.

"No, no," she coughed. "Fine. I'll be fine," she said, feebly waving her hand.

Tony held her hand. "You sure?"

"Sure, I'm fit as, uh, a fiddle," she said, trying to smile. The attempt made Tony want to cry. He held the tears back and smiled at his aunt.

"God will take care of me, don't worry."

Tony tried to look encouraging. He didn't share his aunt's faith.

"I'll clean up the mess," he said.

She nodded, too tired to argue.

After he cleaned up the spilled popcorn, Tony went into the kitchen. He needed to talk to somebody. He picked up the phone and dialed Pam's house. The phone rang and rang.

Nobody was home.

He pushed down the hook and then dialed Bone's number. The phone started to ring.

Bone felt the knife hit him again. This time in the stomach. Part of him knew that the game wasn't real; he wasn't going to die if he was hit again. But another part of him was scared that if the knife found the mark again, he would really die.

He raised the club and hit the troll again. A bell rang when the blow landed. He struck again and once again the bell rang. Bone didn't remember a bell ringing in the game. He struck again. The bell didn't ring.

108

The troll fell to one knee. Bone continued his on-slaught, striking again and again. The bell rang after a few blows, then stopped. The Bull troll suddenly rose to its feet, trembled and roared, then disintegrated.

The bells rang again. Incessantly.

Bone smiled and ran over to free the girls.

He hit the chains with the club and they shattered with the first blow since he had killed the troll.

"We need you, Bone," they said in normal voices. "Come to the club tonight. We miss you."

"I'll be there," Bone mouthed the words.

The bells rang.

Bone snapped to attention. He looked at the screen and saw that the game was in the pause mode. And then he remembered. He had put the game on hold to rest his eyes. He must have fallen asleep.

The bells rang again and Bone realized that the phone was ringing. He reached over and grabbed the handset off of the hook.

"Hello," he said.

"Hey, man, what's up?"

"Nothing, Tone, except I just had the weirdest day-dream . . ."

Tony interrupted. "Bone, my aunt's really bad," he said his voice strained with worry. "I don't know what to do."

Bone quickly forgot about the dream. "What happened?" he asked earnestly.

As Tony explained how his aunt had fallen and how terrible she looked, Bone's mind wandered back to the room. He saw Ashley and Lori. They were smiling and blowing him kisses. He could almost feel their soft hair against his cheek.

"She's going to die and there's nothing I can do about it," Tony said, wiping the tear that rolled down his cheek.

"Bummin'," Bone said, vaguely aware of his friend on the other end of the line. He saw Ashley wink and lick her lips. He could see her lips mouth the words, "Come on."

"She tries to pretend for my sake, but she and I both know that she isn't going to make it much longer."

"I'll try to make it," Bone whispered to the vision in his mind.

"Bone?"

He heard his name.

"Hey, man, did you hear me?"

"Huh," Bone said, suddenly aware of the phone in his hand.

"Hell, man, I'm pouring my guts out and you're not even paying attention."

"What? Oh, Tone, I'm sorry, I was just thinking about the room at the club . . ."

"What? The room at the club?" Tony's voice grew dark with anger. "Just forget it, jerkoff, I'll see you in school . . . Maybe."

Tony slammed the phone down in Bone's ear.

"Tony, man, I . . ."

Bone hung up the phone. He looked at the television screen and saw the room at the Nightmare Club. Slashes of light came from the faceted glass globe and cut into the mist that suddenly filled his room. Bone

110

took a whiff of the sweet odor and stared at the television. He saw the girls, Ashley and Lori, dancing with each other. They smiled and waved for him to join them. Bone stared at the screen and a smile slowly crept across his face. He quickly forgot about the fight he'd just had with Tony and began to plan that night's escape from his "cell."

Tony couldn't believe what a dork Bone had been. He had called him for a little understanding and the jerk didn't even pay attention. It just wasn't like him. Usually he genuinely cared and helped Tony get over the rough spots in his life, but today, he sounded like he couldn't have cared less about Tony or his aunt. He glanced over at the phone expecting it to ring as Bone called with an explanation and an apology, but he got neither. The phone didn't ring.

He picked it up and dialed Pam's number. The phone rang three times before someone picked up.

"Hello?"

"Mrs. Williams, this is Tony. Is Pam there?"

"Just a minute," the woman said. She held her hand over the phone and called out, "Pam, phone!"

Moments later, Pam picked it up in her room. "Got it," she said.

Her mom hung up.

"Hello?"

"Hey, Pam," Tony said in a lifeless tone of voice.

"What's wrong?" Pam replied, sensing Tony's distress.

"My aunt's doing really badly."

"Oh no. I'm really sorry."

"She looks like she might not make it through the week."

Pam could hear the pain in his voice and it touched her heart. "It must be so hard to deal with."

"Yeah," Tony said as he tried to control his emotions. "I—I tried to call you earlier but you weren't there."

"I know. I was at the store with Mom."

"After I tried to call you, I called Bone to talk to him. I needed to talk to somebody."

"I understand."

"But when I started telling him what was up, he didn't even pay attention. It was really weird. Bone's never been like that before."

"Hmm, maybe, he's, uh, I dunno." Pam could think of no reason for Bone to act that way.

"He really pissed me off! He said he was thinking about that stupid room at the Night Owl Club while I was telling him that I think my aunt's dy-ing," Tony said, his voice cracking.

"Oh, Tony, don't cry," Pam said. Her eyes started to fill with tears.

"First I lose my parents and then I have to lose her," Tony said, trying to hold back his own tears.

"I'm coming over," Pam said.

"No. When Aunt Ann's really sick she doesn't want anybody coming over."

"But you need somebody to talk to," Pam protested softly.

"I—I want you to . . . she's really bad." Tony repeated wanting Pam to come over badly, but not wanting to upset his aunt.

"Tony, please," Pam said. "We could sit outside and talk. I don't even have to see her."

Tony nodded. "Okay."

"I'll be over as soon as I can."

"Thanks, Pam. I, uh, thanks."

Pam thought for a moment that Tony was going to tell her something more, but he didn't.

"See you in a little bit," Pam said. "I love you."

"Bye." Tony said, wiping his eyes. He hung up the phone and stared at it. He wished that he could tell Pam how he felt about her, but he was afraid. Afraid to tell her his feelings, afraid to love her. Anytime he loved someone, something bad happened to them. He loved his parents and they died in a car crash. He loved his aunt and now she was dying of cancer. He wasn't going to curse Pam Williams with his love.

The phone rang.

Bone!

Tony picked up the handset. "Hello?"

"Yes, this is Joe Sprague with Riverside Mortuary. May I speak to Mr. Kelvin Sims please."

"What?"

"May I speak to your dad? I have some important information for him on family plots."

"My dad?" Tony couldn't believe what this guy was saying. His dad had been dead for five years.

"Yes. I have some . . ."

Tony slammed the phone down on the hook. The salesman's call was either some kind of terrible coincidence or someone was playing a sick joke. He turned his thoughts toward Bone Fenimore and anger rose up inside him. He didn't think Bone had called, but it reminded him of his friend's penchant for practical jokes.

A short while later, Pam knocked on the door.

"Hey, Tone," she said kissing him.

He smiled and they went outside to talk.

Bone decided that his best route of escape was to wait until his mom and dad were in the living room, then sneak out the back door. He had already parked his bike in the bushes in back of the house so that he could just pedal across his neighbor's yard and then go on to the club. He would arrange his quilt person just like he had done the other time. Once he got to the club, he would wait until at least midnight before coming home. That way he could spend more time with his friends *and* be sure that his mom and dad were asleep when he made his surrepticious entry back into the house.

Bone kept glancing at his watch, waiting for the right moment to make his escape. Occasionally, he would think about Tony and their earlier discussion about his aunt, but visions of the club kept clouding his recollection of the conversation.

A tasteless dinner came and went.

As Bone cleared the table, his father came into the dining room. "Bone, do you have any homework to do tonight?"

"Yeah, a little, I was planning on doing it and then hitting the sack. I'm beat."

"I want you to help me in the garage," Dad said.

"Dad, I've got homework."

"You said a little and besides it'll only take a half hour or so. I need you to hold up a couple of sheets of pegboard while I screw them into the wall and then I want you to help me hang my tools."

"Man," Bone whined in a futile effort of protest.

"Come out to the garage when you get done in here," his father said as he left the room.

"Man, this sucks," Bone said, thinking of the girls at the club.

Just then, a disturbing notion struck him. How did he know the girls were even going to be at the club tonight? They hadn't told him. So how did he know?

Mrs. Fenimore came into the dining room and watched Bone staring at a dish.

"Hey, zombie, wake up," she said.

Bone jumped and then turned on his mom, "Don't do that crap!" he said angrily.

His mother was too startled to do anything but apologize, "I'm sorry. I didn't mean to scare you."

Bone stared at her and then mumbled something that sounded like "S'okay."

A waft of his mother's perfume drifted past him and the scent reminded him of the sweet aroma of the room. Bone smiled.

The abrupt change frightened his mother. "Are you okay?"

"Fine," Bone said. The smell meant that the girls would be there. He didn't know how he knew, he just did. "I gotta go help Dad."

"Okay. I'll finish up," she said, with a concerned expression on her face.

Bone nodded and left the dining room.

He went through the door to the garage where his dad was holding up the pegboard against the spot on the wall where he wanted to put it.

"Hey, come here and hold this," Dad said.

Bone glanced at the clock on the wall, cursed to himself, then did as he was told.

As his dad drilled the holes in the wall and screwed the board to the wall, Bone looked over at the clock again. Eight-thirty. He wanted to leave. Visions of escaping to the room filled his head. He looked over at the balpine hammer sitting on the work bench and thought how easy it would be to hit his dad on the head and knock him unconscious.

The hammer loomed large. He could feel the smooth wooden handle. Feel the cold metal head.

"Hey, hold it straight," his dad said, interrupting Bone's thoughts about the hammer. "Pay attention."

Bone looked at his dad. "I am, Dad," he said coldly.

"Well, then hold it straight."

Bone glanced at the clock and then the hammer. A trickle of sweat dripped into his eye. He looked at the back of his dad's head and thought how easy it would be. Just pick up the hammer and bring it down on his father's head. That's all. Just hit the old man once and then Bone could be on his way to the club. In fact, if he took the hammer inside, he wouldn't have to worry about his mom either. Bone could have full rein of the house and go to the club whenever he wanted.

"There," his dad said. "Finished."

116

Bone snapped to attention. His morbid thoughts blurred and vanished. A moment later he was unable to recall what he had been thinking.

"Well, you can get to that homework now," his dad said.

"Homework?"

"You haven't forgotten?" his dad asked, sarcastically.

"I'll get right on it."

"Good," Dad said, then added, "thanks for your help."

"No problem," Bone replied as he left the garage and went into the kitchen through the side door. When he got inside, he noticed that he was drenched with sweat.

Bone went upstairs and got ready to go. He had wanted to wear the same clothes to allay suspicion in case his parents saw him before he left, but they were soaked with sweat. He changed, then tossed his damp clothes into the laundry hamper. While Bone was fixing the bed to look like he was in it, he wondered if his dad was going to stay in the garage. If so, it would mess up his plans. The bike was right outside the door leading from the garage to the backyard. He might hear him or see him.

He went back downstairs and looked in the living room. His mom was in there watching television. His dad was not. He must still be in the garage.

"Get it all done?" a voice asked behind Bone.

Startled, he jumped.

"Sorry," his dad said, "didn't mean to surprise you."

"That's okay. Are you going to watch television?"

"I thought I might. You get your homework done?"

"Yep. I told you there wasn't much. You gonna watch that show on the Gulf War tonight?"

"Since when have you taken an interest in world affairs?"

"I haven't. I just thought it was something you might like."

"It is. And yes I'm going to be watching it."

"I'm going to bed. I'll see you in the morning."

"It's only nine."

"I know. I'm beat though."

"Okay, 'night."

" 'Night."

Bone watched his dad go into the living room. He acted like he was going upstairs, but veered off into the kitchen. The teenager was glad that his dad hadn't noticed the change of clothes. He went through the side door and hurried to where his bike was parked in the bushes. He pulled it out of its hiding place, jumped on the seat, and started to pedal across the backyard. He hit the street and started down Old Wilson Highway toward Thirteen Bends Road and the Night Owl Club.

When Bone got to the club, he went inside and hurried directly to the room. He didn't bother to look around for the girls; he knew where they would be.

As Bone opened the door to the stairwell, a cold wind blew past him. He shivered, but took no notice. He bounded down the stairs, stopped at the midpoint platform, and then approached the door to the room. Bone grabbed the cold doorknob and opened the door.

When he stepped inside the room, he was momentarily taken aback. The room was as crowded as usual, but it looked different. Older. Not as fresh. The globe was cracked. Spears of light sliced through the fog at odd angles distorting his perspective, making the room look slightly out-of-whack. For a moment, Bone was overcome with a sense of dread. It was as if he had stepped into a nightmare. He saw Ashley and Lori, with their backs turned toward him, sitting at the table.

"Hey, Lor . . ." Bone stopped in mid-word as Lori turned his way. There was something wrong with her face. It looked drawn as if she had lost a lot of weight. Her usually smooth skin looked leathery like a mummy he had seen on a National Geographic television special. Bone felt bony fingers of fear dance up his spine and grab the back of his neck.

"Hey, look it's Bone," Bob Wisniski shouted from across the room.

Bone turned his way and saw the teenager coming toward him.

"Hey, Bone," Lori shouted.

Bone turned back to Lori. She waved and smiled. She looked as pretty as ever.

"Boneman, what's happening?" Bob asked, clapping Bone on the back.

"Nothing much," Bone replied, as he walked over to the table to join the girls.

"Hi," Ashley said. "We weren't expecting you tonight."

"I got bored at home," Bone said. "And I figured

119

you guys missed me."

"Oh we did," Lori said. "We missed you a lot, didn't we, Ash?"

"A whole lot."

"Hey, Bone, what do you think about old Alvin Merritt going crazy?" Bob asked. "Pretty keen, huh?"

"Yeah," Bone agreed as he turned toward the teenager.

Wisniski's cheeks seemed to droop revealing red-rimmed eyes.

Bone heard deep laughter from the back of the room. He looked, expecting to see Jake Demos sitting in the corner of the room. But he was wrong.

It wasn't Demos. The man was shorter. His hair darker.

"Hey, Bone, what do you think of Old Alvin Merritt going crazy?" Bob asked, again. "Pretty keen, huh?"

Bone turned back toward Bob, "You just asked me that, and I just said it was."

"I know you did." Bob smiled a toothy grin. "I was just messing with you. A little dejà vu." The stocky teen laughed loudly and something fell out of his mouth. He picked it up off the table top.

"Lost my Chicklet," he said, as he put the piece of unchewed gum back into his mouth.

Chicklet? Bone thought. He didn't see a Chicklet. That was a tooth!

"Bone, let's dance," Lori said, before Bone had a chance to gather his thoughts. "I feel like dancing."

The deep laughter erupted from the shadowy corner again, further disorienting Bone. He turned, but couldn't make out who was there.

"Bone, come on," Lori insisted, "this is my favorite fast song."

Bone was bewildered. He shook his head and took a deep breath. Then he sighed. "Hold on, I'm a little dizzy."

"Take another deep breath," Ashley said, smiling.

Bone glanced at her. Her hair seemed to be matted and there was something wrong with her eye. He gulped a breath of air and then another. He began to feel better.

"Are we gonna dance or not?" Lori asked.

Bone stood and looked around the room. It was pristine. Beautiful.

"Of course," he said, taking Lori by the hand and leading her out onto the dance floor. His sense of dread faded as he danced with Lori. He breathed in more of the mist as he danced and felt wonderful.

Bone didn't experience any more of the strange distortions of the room or his friends' appearances. The rest of the night was spent having fun entertaining the gang and dancing with the girls.

At around midnight, Bone left the club to get back home. He vowed that he would be back the next night even though he knew he was pressing his luck sneaking out so often in such a short period of time. But it was worth the risk to be the life of the party and to be wanted. Well worth it.

He got on his bike and started down the winding road for home.

Six

It was morning. Bone bounced down the stairs. He was in a great mood. Last night had been wonderful. Once again he was the life of the party. Not only did he get the laughs, he got the girls! And he had even made it back to his room without getting caught. He couldn't wait to go back tonight.

Bone went into the dining room where breakfast was on the table.

"Good morning," Bone said cheerfully.

"Morning," Bone's mom said, then forced a smile. "Where's Dad?"

"He had to leave early," his mom said in a soft voice. Again she forced a smile.

Bone sensed that something was wrong. "What's wrong, Mom?"

"I have some bad news."

Bone felt his stomach muscles tighten.

"Tony's aunt died last night," Mrs. Fenimore said.

Bone felt a hot wave of emotion sweep over him. "When?" he said.

"Tony called about ten."

"Ten," Bone said dully. At ten, Bone had been

cracking jokes at the club.

"I was going to wake you up, but I figured I would wait until morning so you could sleep. I know news like that would've kept you awake."

"Thanks," Bone mumbled. He was stunned. Suddenly he remembered the phone call from his friend. Hadn't Tony said something about his aunt being really bad?

And you were thinking about having fun with the girls in the room. Bone's conscience reminded him. *Remember? You spaced and Tony hung up.*

The thick taste of guilt coated Bone's mouth. He felt sick.

"Tony's staying over at the Williams' house. I asked him if he wanted to stay with us for a few days until his uncle came home. Tony said he'd be over this afternoon."

"Good," Bone said barely aware of what she had said. "I — gotta call him."

Bone got up and went to the phone to call his friend. He took it off the hook, but then realized that he didn't have Pam's phone number and that it was unlisted.

"Man," he said as he slammed the phone back on the hook.

Bone turned to his mom. "How'd he sound last night?"

"He sounded tired. But I think he was also a little relieved that she wasn't suffering anymore."

Bone nodded. "Mom, do you think I could miss school today so I can go see him? He needs somebody to talk to, don't you think?"

"I think under the circumstances it would be okay."

"Thanks." Bone started to leave.

"Hold on, honey, eat something before you go. You need a good breakfast."

"Okay." Bone nodded and sat down at the table. He stabbed a couple of pancakes, put them on his plate, then covered them with syrup.

After he forced himself to eat, Bone got up from the table and went to his room to get dressed.

The shroud of guilt weighed heavily upon him as he went back downstairs. His mom was waiting at the bottom of the steps. She held her keys in her hand.

"Come on, I'll give you a ride to the Williams'. You know how to get there?"

"Yeah," Bone said.

He followed his mom out to the car.

Bone opened the passenger's side door and slid into the seat as his mother entered the driver's side.

"Terrible thing, cancer," his mom said, as she started the car.

"Yeah," Bone agreed. Suddenly, a wave of panic swept over him. What if Tony didn't want to see him? From what Bone could recall of their phone conversation, Tony had been pretty upset with him. Maybe Tony would tell him to get out of his sight.

"Which way?" Mrs. Fenimore asked.

"Left," Bone said.

His mother turned the car and Bone suddenly realized that they were going to have to drive past the Night Owl Club. Anticipation and guilt fought for control of his emotions. For some reason, Bone thought he might see Ashley and Lori outside the club. He had no cause for such a belief, but he hoped anyway.

"I hate this road," Mrs. Fenimore said, referring to Thirteen Bends.

Bone nodded absently as they made their way toward the club.

There it is, Bone thought when he saw the building in the distance. During the day, the club looked like a condemned building from a movie about the end of the world. The brick walls were dirty. There was no sign to indicate that the club was open for business. The only indication that the building wasn't deserted was the blue bulb above the door burning ineffectually against the glare of the morning sun. There were no cars in the dirt parking lot. The trees surrounding the club looked as dead as the building. What had made him think he would see the two girls standing outside such a forbidding place?

"You really go there to have fun?" his mother asked, interrupting Bone's thoughts.

"It's not so bad inside," he replied as he pictured the room downstairs. "It's pretty nice really."

"I bet," she said skeptically.

As the club faded into the black limbs of the distant trees, Bone turned his attention back to his friend. He began to look for the turnoff to the Williams' subdivision.

"This is it," Bone said when he saw the sign for Briarwood Estates.

"Turn here?"

"Yeah," Bone said.

His mom flicked on the turn signal and steered the

car past the entrance to the subdivision.

"Which way?"

"Straight. They live in the last house on the left."

Mrs. Fenimore drove down the street to the last house and pulled into the driveway.

"Thanks, Mom."

"Will you be able to get a ride home?"

"Yeah, we'll probably take Tony's van back to the house."

"Oh, right. Well, you be good and tell Tony I'm sorry about his aunt."

"I will. Thanks, Mom," Bone said. He leaned over and kissed his mom.

Surprised by the sudden expression of emotion, she rubbed her cheek and smiled.

"See you later," Bone said.

"Bye-bye," she said, as she put the car in gear and started to back out of the driveway.

Bone waved to his mom as she drove away to work. He went to the front door of the Williams' house and rang the doorbell.

Mrs. Williams answered.

"Hi, Mrs. Williams, is Tony Sims here?"

"Come on in, uh . . . ?" Bone could tell she was searching for his name and coming up blank.

"Bone. Bone Fenimore."

"Oh, right, I'm sorry. You were here for Pam's birthday party last August."

"Yes, ma'am."

"Tony's in the living room with Pam. I'm sure he'll be glad to see you."

Bone nodded and hoped she was right. After yesterday's phone conversation, he could only hope.

"Hey, Tony," Bone said.

"Hey, man," Tony said. He looked drawn and tired. It was as though he had aged overnight.

Bone felt a lump come to his throat. "I, uh . . ." He cleared his throat. "I'm really sorry about your aunt, man."

"Thanks," Tony said as he looked away and wiped his eyes.

Bone walked over and sat beside him. "Man, I feel like dog turd about yesterday when you called. I don't know . . ."

"Forget it, man, you're here now."

"Well, I was a total wad. And I'm real sorry." He put his hand on Tony's shoulder. He looked over at Tony's girlfriend.

"Hey, Pam," Bone said in a low voice.

"Hi," she said, with a sad expression on her face.

"How did it happen?" Bone asked.

"She just went," Tony said, in a hollow voice.

Pam told the story. "We were outside talking last night until about nine o'clock. We got cold so we went inside to say goodbye. His aunt was on the couch. She looked really bad so we called the ambulance and they took her to the hospital. But it was too late."

"At least she won't be in pain anymore," Bone said, taking a cue from his mother.

"Yeah," Pam said.

Tony nodded dully as if he wanted to believe the statement, but didn't.

At that point, the conversation stalled. There was nothing else to say. Bone and Pam just sat there on the couch and tried to comfort Tony with their presence.

They should've been at school talking about class or the football game or who was dating who, the realities of high school life. Instead, the three teenagers were sitting in a morbidly quiet living room dealing with the ultimate reality — death.

At around two o'clock, Bone volunteered to go to Tony's house and get his clothes so that his grieving friend wouldn't have to confront the memories until he was ready. Tony thanked him and gave Bone the keys to the van and the house.

Bone drove Tony's van to his friend's home and parked it in the driveway. He got out and examined Tony's home. For the first time, Bone noticed that the house wasn't in the best of shape. The blue paint had faded into a dirty grey and was chipped in places. One window had a long crack stretching from one side to the other. The grass was patchy and brown. Grimly, Bone thought that the house looked as dead as its owner.

When he stepped into the Sims' home, Bone was surprised by how cold it was. He shouldn't have been surprised since no one was home and the heat was off, but the room seemed unnaturally chilly. He shivered and went over to the stairs leading to the attic. Tony had told him that a suitcase was there. He opened the door, pulled down the creaky stairs and secured them. Then he took a step. Something moved above him. Bone jumped back from the sound. After listening for a moment and hearing nothing more, he again started up the stairs.

Abruptly, something came darting out of the dark above him and landed on Bone. Bone let out a little shout as he swatted a mouse from his shoulder. Bone chased the mouse until it disappeared in a pile of old newspapers stacked next to the wall.

"Stupid thing," Bone said angry at himself for being scared of a little mouse. He climbed up the stairs, turned on the lone light bulb in the attic, and stepped up into the room.

The attic was cramped and packed with old junk. The light fought a losing battle against the darkness. Dust tingled his nostrils as he breathed in the musty odor of the attic. The reek of age was just what he had expected except that underneath the musty smell was another odor, a sweet smell that was vaguely familiar. Bone sniffed the air to capture the aroma more clearly, but the sweet smell was gone. He shrugged and began to look for the suitcase.

As Bone searched the small room, he saw something in the corner. It was partially hidden by an old blanket. It wasn't a suitcase, but it did pique Bone's curiosity. He made his way over to the corner trying to figure out what it was. Bone reached in and grabbed the yellowish white object. He pulled it out and then almost dropped it when he saw that it was a small skull.

"What the hell?" he said, as he examined the skull. It looked human, but was too small to be a man or a woman's. The other alternative was . . .

No, it couldn't be that. It must be a monkey's skull

or something, Bone told himself. He put the skull back where he found it and hurriedly found the suitcase. "Get me out of here!" he exclaimed.

Bone went into Tony's room and packed some clothes for him to wear. As Bone reached into the closet to grab a pair of Reeboks, he couldn't help thinking about the skull. So small and yet so human looking. What was it doing up there?

Satisfied that he had enough clothes to last Tony for a week, he closed the bag and fastened it shut. He picked it up and left the room. Discovering that skull had given Bone a case of the willies and he couldn't wait to get out of the cold house. He hurried to the front door and outside, shutting and locking the door. Then he carried the case to the van, took one last look at the dilapidated house and drove back to the Williams' home.

When Bone returned, Tony was asleep and Pam was in the kitchen making herself a cup of hot chocolate.

"You want a cup?" Pam asked as Bone joined her in the kitchen.

"Sure," Bone said.

Pam poured a litle more milk into the sauce pan.

"How's Tony?" Bone asked.

"I think he's gonna be okay."

"Man, this sucks."

"It does bigtime," Pam concurred.

"Hey, Pam do you know if Tony's gonna have to make the funeral arrangements?"

"Tony's aunt had everything all taken care of beforehand. She left explicit directions with some guy named Goodfellow. I guess he's her attorney."

"Good, that would really suck if Tony had to do all that crap."

"No doubt," Pam stirred the milk, making sure it didn't burn.

Bone started to tell Pam about the skull he had found, but decided to keep his mouth shut. It was probably from some science project or something. Maybe when Tony felt better he would ask him about it.

"Here's your hot chocolate," Pam said.

"Thanks," Bone said.

"Think I could get a cup of that?" Tony said as he came into the room. He had awakened and smelled the scent of the hot cocoa.

Pam smiled. "Sure," she said, handing him her cup.

"No, I don't want yours."

"Go ahead. I'll make another cup. It only takes a minute for the milk to get warm."

Tony took the cup and sipped some of the liquid. "Oww, I burned the roof of my mouth."

"That's why they call it 'hot' chocolate," Bone said.

"Really," Tony said. "Gee, thanks for the info, Bone."

Bone and Pam laughed. Both were glad to see Tony kidding around with them.

"That's what I'm here for—to keep you informed," Bone added.

Pam heated up some more milk and the threesome went into the living room to watch television. They spent the rest of the afternoon watching reruns like "Gomer Pyle" and "Bewitched" and talking about people at school.

131

At around four, Bone suggested that he and Tony leave for his house so that Tony could get settled into the guest room. Pam agreed.

"Call me later if you want to," Pam said, taking Tony's hand.

"Okay," Tony replied.

"You gonna be okay?"

"Sure. I just got a lot of stuff to work out."

Pam nodded and kissed him. "I love you," she whispered in his ear.

"I — you're the best, Pam," Tony said. He just couldn't say those three words.

Pam tried not to look disappointed, but Tony's lack of affection hurt her.

"Well, let's go, Tone," Bone said, noticing the uncomfortable gap in the conversation.

"Okay," Tony said.

When he got to the door, he took Pam in his arms, and kissed her. Bone looked away and then went to the van to let them have their privacy.

After another long kiss, Tony said goodbye to Pam and came out to join his friend. They got into the van and were soon on the way to the Fenimores' two-story home.

Once they got to Bone's home, Tony carried his suitcase into the house. Bone followed.

The house was empty. Bone's mom and dad hadn't gotten home from work yet.

The two teenagers started up the stairs.

"I guess you're staying in the spare bedroom," Bone said.

"Cool."

"You know where it is, don't you?"

"Sure. I'll go unpack," Tony said as he reached the top of the stairs and started to go down the hall. When he got about halfway to the room, he turned. "Hey, man, thanks for coming today."

Bone smiled. "No prob. You'd be there for me if something bad happened."

"Yeah," Tony nodded, turned, and went up the stairs to the spare room.

Bone went into his bedroom and was surprised to see that his television and the video game were on. He was sure that he hadn't turned them on that morning.

So how come they were on now?

He looked at the screen and saw that the game was in the final stage. The room at the club was displayed. Bone saw a fine mist spread from the picture on the screen. It seemed to penetrate the glass screen and drift toward him. Bone was frightened and was about to call out for Tony when the mist hit him. The sweet smell overwhelmed him. He staggered and almost fell. But soon the mist filled his lungs. He felt lightheaded. Almost giddy. He looked at the screen and saw the girls chained to the wall.

"Help us," they said, in their synthetic voices. "We need you."

He bent down and picked up the controller. It felt like a club.

The door opened.

"Hey, what time do you usually ea . . ." Tony stopped in mid-word when he saw the odd look on his friend's face. "Bone?"

Bone turned and stared at Tony. Only it wasn't Tony

133

standing there at the door. It was an ugly troll with one eye lower than the other and sharp nasty teeth jutting out of a misshapen mouth.

And the horrible thing was coming to get him. Bone raised the club over his head.

"Bone? What's wrong?"

Bone took a step toward Tony.

"Hey."

Abruptly, the troll's face shifted and it became Tony Sims. Bone shook his head. "Sorry, Tone, you scared me."

"Man, I thought for a second you were gonna throw that controller at me."

Bone looked at the controller in his hand and forced a laugh. "No. You just surprised me."

"Sorry. I was just wondering what time you guys usually eat dinner."

"Around six," Bone said, glancing at the screen. Traces of the sweet aroma of the mist lingered in the bedroom. Lori and Ashley were beckoning him.

"What are you looking at?" Tony asked.

"Huh?" Bone responded as Ashley blew him a kiss.

"You're staring at the screen like something was there."

The picture on the screen faded right before Bone's eyes. He rubbed his eyes and looked away.

"You okay?" Tony asked.

"Just a little tired I guess."

"I know what you mean. That little snooze I took this afternoon didn't do a thing for me. I'm still beat."

"I don't doubt it. You've been through a lot with your aunt and all that stuff."

134

Tony smiled sadly. "I miss her already, Bone."

Bone didn't know what to say. Sixteen-year-old class clowns weren't at their best in situations dealing with grief. So he said nothing and just listened, which ended up being exactly the right thing to do.

Tony sat on the bed and started talking about all the things that were bottled up inside him. As he spoke softly about the good times he'd had with his aunt in the past, Bone tried to focus his attention on what his friend was saying. But his eyes kept drifting toward the screen. Vague images of the room drifted in and out. Ashley's face would appear, blow a kiss and then vanish. Lori would smile and beckon him to dance.

"She was really pretty," Tony said, remembering his aunt on the night she and his uncle went out for their tenth anniversary. "Really pretty."

"Yeah, she was," Bone said, as the images on the screen called out to him He could hear Ashley saying, "We're waiting for you, Bone. Come on."

"I'm just glad she went fast. The doctor said he didn't think she suffered when she went."

"That's good," Bone said. He wished his friend would just shut up about his dead aunt and leave the room.

"Bone, what's going on?" Tony said, shaking his friend's arm. He was concerned about the distant expression on Fenimore's face. "What are you thinking about?"

Bone's eyes focused on his friend. He lied. "I was just thinking how nice your aunt was." Nice and dead, Bone added laughing to himself. Now get the

135

hell out of here and leave us alone.

A door closed downstairs. Footsteps climbed the stairs.

"Hey, guys," Mrs. Fenimore said as she came into the room. "How are you doing, Tony?"

"Pretty good I guess."

"Well, anything you need you just ask," she added, smiling gently.

Tony returned her smile with one of his own. "Thanks, Mrs. Fenimore."

"I have to go and get dinner ready. You like pot roast and little potatoes?"

"Yeah. Sounds good."

"Good, then I'm going to go get out of these work clothes and get comfortable." She smiled and looked at her son who was staring at the television screen. "Harold, aren't you going to say hello?"

Bone looked away from the image of Ashley calling to him. "Hi, Mom."

"That's better," she said. "Now, I'll call you when dinner's ready."

"Okay," Bone said, scarcely aware of her comment. He turned back to the screen, but Ashley was gone.

Curious, Tony watched him and wondered what Bone found so interesting about the blank screen.

"Hey, Bone, you're zoning again," Tony said.

"Oh, sorry," Bone said.

"You know something?"

"What?" Bone said absently. Lori had just appeared again and was beckoning to him.

"I really appreciate you listening to me, man. It feels good to talk about my aunt. Get some stuff off

136

my chest. Most guys would've, y'know, blown me off or something cause, well, death is hard to talk about. But you really care. You're a real pal and I want to thank you." He put his hand on Bone's shoulder.

Warmth radiated from Tony's hand as it rested on Bone's shoulder and Bone noticed that Lori's smiling face changed. For a moment, her lips curled back like those of an angry dog. Her eyes glared red and then she faded leaving a frightened Bone in the wake of the change. Bone turned to his friend and thoughts of the room at the club vanished as quickly as they had come. He smiled at his friend, but diffused the emotional scene with customary humor.

"We're closer than pals, remember?" Bone tugged on the chain around his friend's neck reminding him of the joke with the necklace and the funny bone charm. It seemed so long ago that he had played that joke. He put his arm around Tony. "We're going steady."

"Man, I'm gonna hurl," Tony said, pushing his friend away.

Bone laughed. "Let's go downstairs and watch 'Gilligan's Island' or something on the big TV?"

"Okay, I need something to numb my head for a little while."

As they got up and headed for the door, Tony stopped and turned to his friend. "I really do want to thank you, man."

Bone smiled sheepishly. "That's okay, dude. Like I said you'd do the same thing for me."

Tony smiled. "Yeah, now let's go watch Gilligan mess up their chances of leaving the island for the hundredth time."

"Thousandth time, but who's counting," Bone said.

The boys went downstairs as Bone's dad came through the front door.

"Hey, Tony, how are you doing?"

"Pretty good, Mr. Fenimore."

"I was really sorry to hear about your aunt," Mr. Fenimore said with genuine feeling. "She was a nice lady."

"Yeah, she was," Tony replied.

"Well, I just want you to know that you're welcome to stay with us for as long as you want."

"Thank you."

Bone's dad nodded and went up the stairs to get out of his "monkey suit," as he called it, and into some comfortable clothes. The boys went into the living room to watch television until dinner.

After stuffing themselves, Tony and Bone went upstairs. They talked for a little while, but soon fatigue from the long day of emotional turmoil caught up with them. Tony went to the bathroom and brushed his teeth before going into the guest room and dropping into bed. Bone did the same thing in his room.

As he reached over and turned off the lamp beside his bed, Bone heard a sound outside his window. He clicked the light back on, but saw nothing. He waited to see if he could see what it was outside the window, but nothing appeared. He told himself it must have just been the house settling. He clicked off the light again and tried to go to sleep.

When he closed his eyes, he saw Lori and Ashley standing beneath his window. The vision was so clear that he almost got up and went to the window to see if they were there. They were waving at him. He felt his hand raise as he waved back to the girls. He smiled and drifted off to sleep.

A single tap struck the window.

Bone stirred.

Something else hit the glass pane.

Bone's eyes snapped open. He looked toward the window and in the light of the moon saw a small object strike it again. His first thought was that it was a beetle or some kind of bug, but that wasn't the right sound. The tap made by the object hitting the glass pane had a hard sound to it. He figured it was more likely a rock by the sound of the click when it hit.

Abruptly, a thought came to him.

No, it couldn't be. Logic contradicted the improbable notion.

But Bone knew that he was right. He knew who was out there. He just knew that Ashley and Lori were outside on the lawn throwing rocks up at his room.

But it couldn't be them, his logical side argued unable to remain silent in the face of such an improbability. How could they know where he lived or what room was his? And why would they be there at, he glanced at the clock, twelve-fifteen?

I know it's them, Bone countered as he threw back the covers and got up out of bed. His logical side would hold no sway that night. He went over to his dresser and grabbed a pair of shorts so that the girls wouldn't see him in his underwear. He put them on then went to the window to see what his adventurous girlfriends wanted.

Smiling, he opened the window and looked down on the lawn. His heart jumped into his throat when he saw Bull Merritt glaring at him from below the window. His expression reflected hatred and madness. Improbably, the teenager charged the house and tried to scale the walls. He climbed about five feet, clawing at the wall trying to get at Bone, but gravity yanked him back to the ground.

Frightened, but fascinated by the display, Bone watched as Merritt assaulted the wall again and again. Each time he seemed to climb further and further up the wall before dropping back down. He would get what seemed to be an impossible hold, then move up a few feet before he would lose the hold and fall. The single-minded fury of the assault was chilling to watch and yet Bone knew he was in no danger. It was like watching a scary movie to him. Bone could picture Bull scaling the wall and it would scare him, but he also knew that it could never happen and so the fear was safe to experience.

Suddenly, Merritt stopped his assault and looked up at the window. He smiled in a way that made Bone's skin crawl. The insane teenager took off running around the house.

Bone's fear escalated rapidly because Merritt had gone from a visible impotent spectacle to an unseen adversary of dangerous intent. Bone ran to the door to call out for his dad, but when he opened the door, someone was there. Bone's whole body tingled with fright and sickness when he saw the bloody face of his friend, Tony.

Bull had already been in the house! He had been at

the window just to divert Bone's attention!

Tony fell to the ground brushing Bone and trailing blood down his bare chest.

"Tony!" Bone shouted.

There was no response. Tony had used the rest of his energy to get to Bone's room to warn him. He was dead.

"Tony, man, don't be dead," he cried.

"Too bad, dipwad," a cold voice intoned. "He made like a ghost for real." Bull's twisted laughter didn't sound even vaguely human.

Bone scampered backward on the heels of his hands. His stomach muscles cramped with fear.

"Why, Bull? Why?" he cried.

Merritt ignored him and said in a pleasant conversational tone, "Hey, dipwad, do you have any idea how hard your mom's head was. It took me six hits with this . . ." He held up a mallet. ". . . to get any brains to come out."

Bone's stomach lurched, and he vomited.

Bull laughed wildly and stepped over the still body of Tony Sims. "I told you nobody ever wins when they mess with me."

Bull's words sounded disconnected as if they were coming from somewhere other than his mouth. The effect chilled Bone and he realized in misery that he was about to wet his pants.

If it wasn't for his aching bladder, Bone would never have escaped from the nightmare. He lurched up, realized how close he was to disaster, threw back the covers and then ran into the bathroom to relieve himself. He wiped his sweaty face with a towel and tossed it in the dirty clothes bin, then he climbed back into the bed and tried to get back to sleep.

Bone wondered what might have triggered the dream about Merritt, but could think of nothing. In fact, he hadn't thought about the fullback since he had heard about his admission to the mental hospital.

At around three, he finally drifted back to sleep.

Seven

The next day began uneventfully.

In the morning, Bone's mom came into her son's room and asked him if he would stay home with Tony that day. She knew from losing her mother that the second and third days were sometimes worse than the first. You started to miss your loved ones and needed someone there to be with you. Bone readily accepted the request.

After Bone's parents left for work, the boys spent the morning watching television and talking.

At around noon, they had lunch then went outside and shot the basketball for a while before coming back into the house. They went upstairs and into Bone's room where they played a few video games of baseball. After tiring of the game, they went back downstairs to watch television.

Four o'clock rolled around and there was a knock on the door. Bone got up from the couch and went to answer it. When he opened the door, he stood face to face with a short little fat man. Bone's first thought was that Cupid's grandfather had come to visit.

"Hello," the man said. "My name is Goodfellow. I

was told that Tony Sims might be here."

"Oh, yeah, he is," Bone said. "How'd you know that?"

"Mrs. Williams told me," the man said with a kindly smile.

"Oh."

"I am, or rather was, Tony's aunt's attorney. I need to talk to Tony about the arrangements. May I come in?"

"I guess," Bone said. He felt a little uncomfortable letting a stranger in the house, but the man was an attorney and he did have a logical story.

"Tony's in here," Bone said as he walked into the living room. Goodfellow followed.

"Hello, Tony, I'm Mr. Goodfellow," the man said, extending a pudgy hand. Tony shook it.

"I'm here to talk to you about your aunt's will and the requests that she wanted to be executed," he said as he sat in the chair opposite the couch where Bone and Tony were seated.

"You're the attorney?" Tony knew his aunt had a lawyer, but he'd never met him before today.

"Yes. Now, the first thing is that your aunt wanted you taken care of while you attended high school and college. She left you with a trust fund that I will administer until you are twenty-one. The fund will pay for your health insurance, room and board, automobile expenses and allots you two hundred dollars a month for miscellaneous expenditures like movies, dinner and the like. A portion of the trust is set aside for college and will only be used for that purpose. If you don't go to college, you don't get that money. You will receive a monthly check to cover

144

your expenses."

Tony nodded. He thought his Uncle John would be taking care of him, but Tony hadn't seen him in years. Maybe he *should* just live on his own.

"I will represent you at a dependency hearing to determine if it's in your best interest to live alone or with an appointed guardian, your uncle, I believe. I think in your case we will be able to prove that you're responsible enough to live on your own for the next year. If that's what you wish."

Tony shrugged. He didn't know what he wanted yet. He didn't want to decide this second.

"I was instructed to clear out the attic and remove certain items that your aunt designated for charity. I have a crew working on it as we speak."

"What kind of stuff?"

"Oh, nothing that would interest you. Old books and other things of no interest to a teenager I'm sure."

Tony had been in the attic a few times, but all that was up there was junk. It just seemed odd that the man was moving it without his approval, but he guessed the man knew the law. After all, he was an attorney.

Goodfellow cleared his throat. "Now on the funeral arrangements, uh, your aunt wished to be cremated and buried in a private ceremony to be held in the woods lining Cross Road tomorrow at nine. Now I don't want you to take this wrong, but she didn't want you to be there."

"What?" Tony said.

"She expressed the fact that she wanted you to remember her as she was. She didn't want you to remember her as in her words 'a walking corpse.' "

145

"But . . ."

"I am just conveying her wishes. She doesn't want you to attend. She even went so far as to request that if you were seen in attendance that I was to extend my control of your trust fund until your thirtieth birthday."

Tony knitted his brow as Goodfellow continued.

"She left me these photo albums of herself before the illness took her. They are to be your memorial of her."

He handed the albums to Tony. He opened one of them and saw his aunt's smiling face. She was radiant. He had never seen these pictures before that moment. They showed his aunt in beautiful gowns of lace and silk. She glowed.

"Wow," Bone said looking over his friend's shoulder as Tony turned the pages. "She's beautiful, man."

As Tony turned to the last page, Bone's heart jumped. On that page was a picture of Tony's aunt standing in the middle of a ballroom. It was the room from the Night Owl Club! He was sure of it. It was decorated differently, but he was sure that it was the room.

"Tony, man, that's the room at the Night Owl Club. The one I told you about," Bone said, excitedly.

Tony looked at the picture and pulled it out of the plastic cover. He turned it over to see if it said when it was taken.

June 1950. New York City.

"This says it's in New York." Tony flipped the picture back over and looked at it.

Bone also examined it closely and realized that he had been mistaken. The ceiling was higher than the room at the club's was. There were no pillars in the room, either. "It looked like it for a minute."

"Uh, yes," Goodfellow said, "Now there are some other minor details that we need to discuss."

As Goodfellow talked to Tony, Bone's mind wandered back to the picture. He had been sure that it was the room from the club when he first saw the picture.

"Can I look at this again?" Bone asked his friend.

"Sure."

Bone opened the book to the last page and looked at the photo of Tony's aunt. He stared at the picture with his mouth open. It was the room! There were the pillars. The faceted glass globe hanging from the ceiling.

Then he saw something that he couldn't believe. In the corner of the room sitting at the table it was . . .

Bone rubbed his eyes and looked at the picture again.

It was Ashley. She seemed to be looking straight at him. Bone took a deep breath to clear his head and was overwhelmed by the sweet smell emanating from the picture.

He looked over at his friend Tony to see if he smelled the aroma, but Tony didn't even look his way. In fact, he seemed to be sitting far off in the distance. It was as if something had happened to Bone's depth perception. He stared at his friend for a moment, trying to clear his vision.

Bone glanced over at the cherubic old man. The old man turned toward him and smiled.

Bone looked back down at the book and saw that Tony's aunt had started dancing with a handsome man. From the back of the room, Ashley got up from her seat and went out into the dance floor. She started dancing across the floor as though someone were in her arms. The image of this beautiful girl spinning around the room in the long flowing dress was hypnotic. Bone stared at her, feeling her arms around his neck, her hair brushing his cheek. He could smell sweet perfume. He missed her.

"Will I see you tonight?" Ashley said. Although her mouth didn't move, Bone heard the words in his head.

I'll be there, Bone thought.

Ashley smiled and whirled across the floor. Bone understood that she had heard his thoughts. He closed the book.

Goodfellow was just finishing his meeting with Tony. He stood up and shook the young man's hand.

"Thank you, Mr. Goodfellow."

"I will be in touch. Goodbye."

He nodded and left.

"He was pretty nice," Tony said. "I just can't believe some of the things my aunt wanted done. I mean, I know she didn't want to talk to me about this stuff. I stopped trying weeks ago because it just upset her. Maybe I should have tried harder to get her to tell me. It's pretty weird."

"Yeah," Bone said absently.

"Can I have that?" Tony asked, pointing to the album in Bone's hand.

Bone nodded and handed him the book.

"I'm gonna put this up in my room," Tony said.

"Go ahead," Bone said. He was thinking about the club and how he was going to get there that night.

An hour later, Bone's parents arrived home. After changing their clothes, his dad started watching the news, while his mom started preparing dinner—stir fried chicken and vegetables. Tony came downstairs and set the table for her.

Bone went to Tony's room to look at the picture again. To his confusion, the picture was no longer of the room at the club. It was a room in that New York club. Bone closed the book, figuring that Ashley had already gotten her message to him. Then he grabbed something off Tony's dresser that he would need to get to the club later. He went into his room where he stayed until his mother called him for dinner.

The meal was tasty and everyone seemed to enjoy it except Bone who was too busy thinking about going to the room and seeing his friends again.

"That was a great dinner, Mrs. Fenimore," Tony said as he wiped the corner of his mouth with a napkin.

"I'm glad you liked it," she replied.

Tony stood and started to help her clear the table.

"You don't need to do that," Mrs. Fenimore said as she picked up a plate and scraped the leftovers into a used bowl. "Bone will help me."

Bone was dancing with Lori at the club when he heard his name mentioned. He turned his attention toward the voice of his mother. "Huh?"

"Help me clean up the table, will you?"

"Sure," Bone said. He wanted to get the job done so that he could get to the club faster.

"I don't mind helping," Tony said. "Gives me something to do."

Mrs. Fenimore nodded in understanding.

After they cleared the table, Bone and Tony went upstairs.

"Hey, man, I need to ask you for a favor," Bone said.

"What's up?"

"I need to borrow your van."

"Sure, no problem. When do you need it?"

"Tonight."

"Tonight?"

"Yeah, I'm going to the club for a little while."

"I thought your parents didn't let you go out on a school night."

"They don't. But I need to get out. I haven't seen Ashley and Lori in a long time."

"I don't know. I hate the idea of your using the van and then getting caught. Your mom and dad have been pretty cool letting me stay here."

"You could come with me, " Bone said. "We could have a lot of fun."

"Man, my aunt just died. I don't feel like going out."

"But it would get your mind off it."

"I don't think so. Besides, I just don't feel right going behind your mom and dad's backs after they were so nice to me."

"Wait a sec . . ." Bone said, getting angry. "You're not gonna let me use the van?"

"Man, they're letting me stay in their house and so I go and help their son break the rules. It's not too cool."

"Forget cool, Tone, I want to go to the club, and I need a ride."

"Bone, man, I don't know."

Bone got madder. "The girls are expecting me to be there and I'm going."

150

"What do you mean the girls are expecting you? When did you talk to them?" Tony said, wondering why Bone hadn't mentioned the call from the girls. Usually he would have bragged about it.

"What is this? The third degree? I just want to borrow your van, not give you my life history."

Tony was taken aback by Bone's attitude. It wasn't like him. "Chill out, Bone. I was just asking."

"You won't get in trouble if that's what you're worried about. I'll say I took it without you knowing."

"Come on. You're putting me in a bad situation." Tony said.

"I didn't know you were such a wuss," Bone said angrily. "Just forget it, man." He went over and turned on the video game.

The stunned Tony couldn't figure it out. Bone was going off on him for no reason. He started to get a little ticked. His aunt had just died two days ago and now Bone was getting mad at him for not letting him use the van.

"I'm gonna go in my room and chill," Tony said, not wanting the argument to escalate.

Bone nodded as he played the game.

Tony turned and walked out of the room. Bone watched him leave and smiled. He pulled the keys to the van out of his pocket. With or without his friend's permission he was going to the club that night.

Tony called Pam from the phone in the guest room that Bone's mom had plugged in for him.

"Hey," Tony said.

"Hi, Tone, how you doing, sweetie?"

"Okay. I just got in a weird argument with Bone."

"An argument?"

"Yeah. He wanted to borrow my van to go to the club tonight. But his mom and dad don't like him going out on a school night so I know he's sneaking out. They've been so cool to me I just didn't think it would be right to go behind their backs."

"You're right. I can't believe Bone would put you in that position."

"Me, neither. Then he got really pissed when I told him I didn't want to do it. Called me a wuss and wouldn't talk to me."

"That doesn't sound like Bone at all."

"I know. It's totally out of character. Remember the phone call I had with him the day Aunt Ann died. It was like he didn't care about her. As a matter of fact, he was talking about that stupid room at the club. Same as tonight."

"What room?"

"The one at the club I told you about—where he met the girls."

"Oh yeah."

"It's weird, too, how he zones out sometimes almost like he's seeing things. It's just not the Boneman we know."

"No, it's not like him at all."

"Maybe I should go talk to him and apologize."

"I think he should apologize to you, Pam said. "I mean your aunt, just, you know." She didn't know what words to use. Died. Passed on. Went to heaven.

"Maybe he's having trouble knowing what to say to me about stuff now that Aunt Ann's gone. Her death's not something he can make jokes about so he can't really deal with it on his terms."

"Well, maybe it's time he grew up a little."

Tony nodded. "Maybe."

"I miss you, Pam said.

"I miss you too, Pam," Tony said.

"When are you coming back to school?"

"Tomorrow. I can't keep putting it off. Nothing's gonna bring her back."

"When is her funeral?"

"They're having something for her tomorrow. But the attorney says she didn't want me to go. Put it in her will. They're having some special ceremony thing. It's really bizarre, but that's the way she wanted it to be, so I guess I'll just accept it"

"She didn't want you to go?"

"No," Tony said as he explained the reasons for his aunt's request as Mr. Goodfellow had related them.

"I guess it makes sense if those were her reasons," Pam said, although she still found it odd.

"I'm really glad she gave me that photo album. It really does let me remember her the way she would want to be remembered—young and pretty. Oh, man, that reminds me of something else Bone did. He thought one of the pictures in the album was of that room at the Night Owl Club. We turned it over and it said New York City."

"He must have it on the brain."

"I guess. But it's kinda I dunno, scary. I hope he's not losing it like Bull Merritt."

"No way. He just met those girls and they liked him. That's all. I mean he's never had a girlfriend before."

"I guess."

The two continued talking for another half hour. The conversation slowly shifted from concerns about

Bone Fenimore to a discussion about their relationship. Tony really cared about Pam, but talking about their feelings for each other made him feel uneasy. It went back to his experiences of the past. All those he loved had died. He couldn't get that fact out of his mind.

"Well, I have to go," Tony said, uncomfortable with the conversation. "Mrs. Fenimore might want to use the phone."

"Tony, I really care about you, I just want you to know that."

"I know. It's just that I . . . I gotta go."

Pam sensed his discomfort and decided to wait for a better time. She knew that he was still reeling from his aunt's passing. "Okay, I'll see you at school tomorrow."

"I'll meet you by the lockers before class starts."

"Okay. I love you," she said quickly.

"I—I'll see you."

Tony hung up and collapsed on the bed. He glanced at the clock and realized how long he had been talking to Pam.

At ten-thirty, Tony sat up in the bed in the guest bedroom. He was still upset about his earlier argument with Bone and couldn't get to sleep. Maybe if he went and talked to Bone, he could find out what was wrong with him. Getting up out of bed, he slipped on a pair of shorts, left the guest room, and walked down the hallway to Bone's room. Bone was asleep under the covers, and Tony walked over and tapped him.

"Bone?" he whispered as his finger sunk into his friend's body. He jumped back, startled by the softness of his friend's shoulder.

"Bone?" he said a little louder, gingerly nudging his friend's shoulder. It collapsed.

Tony grabbed the covers and saw the quilt that Bone had arranged to simulate his body.

"That dog," Tony said. "He went anyway."

Tony left the room and went back to the guestroom which faced the street. He looked out the window and saw that his van was gone.

"Why'd you bother asking if you were gonna take it?" he asked angrily.

Boy, those girls must be something to get you to lie to your parents and your best friend, Tony thought as he sat on bed and wondered what he should do when Bone got back from the club.

Bone arrived at the Night Owl Club at around nine-forty-five and went straight to the room.

When he opened the door to the room, Bone experienced the same feeling that he'd had the last time he had stepped into the room. A perception that something was wrong, a sense of distortion. The room seemed to tilt a bit. The shafts of light reflected off the globe were bent at odd angles. His friends' faces went from sunken and lifeless to plump and lively in a blink of his eye. He watched the mist spread across the room from the unseen smoke machine like a giant amoeba coming to absorb him. When the sweet smell hit him, he reeled. The room spun for a moment, then settled, and became the happening place that he had come to love.

"Bone's here!" Lori shouted gleefully as she ran across the room and hugged him.

155

"Bone!" Ashley called out, leaving her dance partner standing on the floor. She ran over and hugged him as well.

Bone felt like a conquering king returning from a battle. His subjects gathered around him and he held court. Cracking jokes, dancing, telling stories. Drunk with adoration, he overlooked little rips in his perception like Ashley's nose splitting and repairing itself *(must be a trick of the lights)* or the strange rotten odor of Lori's breath on occasion *(someone was cutting the cheese while he was talking to her and he must have unfortunately associated the smell with her).* These distortions corrected themselves and everything returned to normal with a gulp of the sweet air.

That night, Ashley finally chose to assert herself and claim Bone as her sweetheart. She danced with him on every slow song and held his hand while they sat at the table. Lori asked Bone to dance a couple of times, but Ashley's withering stare signaled that Bone was now her boyfriend and it was hands off. Lori seemed to accept her loss and danced with Bob Wisniski most of the night.

As time rolled past the witching hour and into the morning, Bone looked at his watch and knew that he should get home. He had to get up for school in the morning.

"What's wrong?" Ashley said, seeing Bone's contemplative expression.

"I have school tomorrow so I have to go," Bone said to his girlfriend. "I hate this crap."

"You don't *have* to go," Ashley said coyly.

"Yeah, I do. But I'll be back tomorrow night. You

156

will be here tomorrow night?"

"Of course," Ashley said. "But I wish you'd stay."

Bone looked at his watch and then smiled. "Well, maybe a little while longer."

Bone arrived home at around five o'clock that morning. The exhausted teenager parked the van, got out, and closed the door as softly as he could. He snuck around to the back of the house and quietly entered. He closed the door, locked it, and then stealthfully passed through the house and up the stairs.

Fully clothed, he fell into bed on top of his fabric double squashing it. He closed his eyes and tried to get an hour's shuteye before the alarm slapped him upside the head.

Eight

The morning sky was ominous. Clouds lurked on the horizon. Lightning slashed white leering smiles across gray black faces as malevolent laughter rumbled in the distance.

Tony unlocked the door to the passenger side and then walked around the car to unlock his door. He got in the car and then waited for Bone to climb into the passenger seat. As they started driving toward Cooper High, Tony asked, "You took my van to the club last night, didn't you?"

Immediately, Bone took an offensive stance. "So? I told you I needed to go and since you blew me off I decided to do it anyway and I'm glad I did. I had a great time. I ruled the room."

Tony was once again shocked by his friend's surly attitude, "It doesn't bother you that I didn't give you permission to take my van?"

Bone shrugged. "Not really. I wanted to go and I did. If you were my friend you wouldn't have told me no in the first place."

"What's that supposed to mean?"

"Man, just leave me alone. I'm beat."

"No, I want to know what your problem is."

"My problem is that you tried to keep me from going to the room."

"What?"

"Maybe you're jealous because my new friends think I'm the best."

Tony couldn't believe what he was hearing. It was as if Bone was a victim of the bodysnatchers and been replaced with a duplicate. "Look, I'm glad you got a girl, but I can't believe you're dissing me like this."

Bone squeezed his eyes. "Look, Tone, I'm just tired and cranky, man. I was out until five. We'll talk this afternoon, okay?"

"I'm worried about you, man, you're acting weird. Staying out till five and stuff. I don't know."

"I just lost track of time. And there was no harm done. Mom and Dad didn't find out that I went so it's cool."

Tony shook his head. He didn't feel like arguing anymore.

When they arrived at school, Bone went to his locker and Tony went to his locker. Pam was waiting for him.

"Hi," Pam said, kissing Tony.

"Hi."

"How you doing?"

"Pretty good, I guess. It's just so weird."

"What's weird?"

"I asked Bone why he took the van last night and he acted real funny."

"What do you mean?"

"Real cocky like he didn't care whether I was mad

159

or not," Tony said, then sighed. "He's been acting so weird lately. Ever since he started hanging at that room at the Night Owl Club. I guess having girls pay attention to him is changing him a little."

"I think he's really being selfish. It's a hard time for you and he's going out partying."

"In a way, I don't blame him. I felt like running away from it myself. Bone's just not good at dealing with heavy stuff, I guess."

Pam nodded. "Maybe. But still, taking your van without your permission is kinda crunchy and then starting an argument with you about it . . . I mean, he does know that your aunt's funeral is today, doesn't he?"

"Yeah," Tony said dully.

Pam touched his cheek. "Well, he should respect your feelings. I mean he has to know that it would be on your mind, especially since you're not supposed to go."

"That's something else that's really bothering me. It seems so strange not to go. Like I'm incomplete."

"So why don't you go anyway?"

Tony looked at her. "But my aunt didn't want me to go. She said so in her will."

"You don't think she would understand?" Pam asked, softly.

"She would, I guess, but . . . I don't know."

"What if we just watched from a distance?"

"We?"

"I'll go with you, if you want." She smiled warmly.

Tony returned the smile. "I would like to say good-bye for the last time."

"Then let's go."

"But you never skip."

"There's always a first time."

Tony nodded. "Okay. Let's do it. But I'm not sure exactly where the ceremony's being held. It's somewhere in the woods along Cross Road."

"Well, that's not too long a road. We'll look for parked cars and then try to find them from there."

"Okay. Let's go."

"You think we should take my car in case someone pulls in after us and recognizes your van?"

"Good idea. You don't mind driving?"

"Not at all. Let's go."

It was close to nine when they saw five cars parked alongside Cross Road. Pam pulled her Metro behind a Black Porsche 944. She and Tony got out of the car.

"This must be where they're having the ceremony," Tony whispered as he walked alongside his girlfriend.

"Let's go find them," Pam whispered.

Tony nodded. They walked into the woods and started to search.

After a few minutes, they heard someone's voice, followed by the rhythmic chanting of several voices. Tony pointed in the direction of the voices and he and Pam walked as quietly as they could in that direction. They stopped behind a large tree and peered around each side of it.

Thirty yards away, a group of about ten people stood in a circle around a small wooden box placed in its center. Pam looked at Tony who shrugged. They wondered about the strange garb that the men and women were wearing—black robes with hoods. They moved in a slow swaying pattern as the man in the middle spoke in a strange tongue that sounded like Latin. After the man completed his part of the ceremony, the others would chant in unison. The effect was hypnotic and Tony felt himself starting to sway with the odd chant.

"What are they doing?" Pam whispered as she came around the tree.

"I don't know." Tony said, snapping out of his momentary trance.

"What religion was your aunt?"

"I think she was a Presbyterian, but I never went to church with her so I don't really know."

"Well, this isn't Presbyterian I can tell you that."

"I know. But what is it?"

They looked back around the tree and saw that the man leading the chant had lit a small torch. He waved the torch in the air, speaking in the strange tongue, then touched the flame to the small box. While the man held the torch to the box, a woman with a silver cup stepped forward and tossed the liquid in the cup onto the torch. A flame jumped into the air and the box caught fire. The woman and the man stepped back and watched it burn.

"What the heck are they doing?" Tony whispered to himself.

The white smoke from the box floated into the air casting a pallor over the scene. The smoke gave the ceremony a surrealistic look. Like it was a dream.

Pam came around the tree. "Tony, what do you think's in that box?"

"I don't know. Maybe something my aunt owned or something. I just don't know."

"I wonder if that attorney guy could tell you what was happening?"

"Probably, but then he would know that I came to the ceremony. It affects my aunt's will. I wouldn't get the trust money until I'm thirty instead of twenty-one."

Pam didn't say anything, but she thought that the whole thing was very bizarre. It was almost like . . .

Tony interrupted her thoughts. "Do you think my Aunt Ann's ashes might be in the box?"

"Why would they burn them twice?"

"Why would they be wearing those black robes?" Tony asked.

Pam shrugged. "You may be right."

As the fire burned, the group turned their backs away from it and started walking.

Tony and Pam ducked behind the tree and hoped that they wouldn't be seen.

"Let's go. We don't want them to see our car," Pam said, as she took Tony's hand and started walking quickly back to the car.

Bone couldn't get his mind off of the room. In the room, he was king. Everyone listened to him. Everyone liked him. He wasn't just the class clown. He had a girlfriend who thought he was cute, smart, and strong. It made him feel so good when he was there; better than he had ever felt in his life. He craved those feeling of power and confidence.

As he sat in his stupid English class listening to stupid Mr. Kitchens blab about stupid Nathaniel Hawthorne, he realized that he needed those emotions to feel alive. Everything else seemed dull and inane next to the feelings he experienced when he was in the room. In the room, he wasn't just another student trying to stay awake while a boring teacher taught him things he didn't need to learn. In the room, he was the big man on campus and all the things he had always wanted to be.

He shook his head as he watched Mr. Kitchens pacing in front of the blackboard.

"In *The Scarlet Letter,* Reverend Dimmesdale was revered as saintly by the parishioners, while Hester Prynne was . . ." Mr. Kitchens stopped and stared as Bone stood up and started walking for the door. "What do you think you're doing, Harold?"

"You're boring me to death," he said, as he opened the door.

The class cracked up.

"Knock it off" Kitchens said as he followed Bone out the door.

"Hold on, Fenimore," he said, grabbing Bone by the arm.

"Let me go, old man," Bone hissed as he wrenched his arm free.

"You get to the vice principal's office right now!" The flustered teacher shouted.

Bone laughed. "Sure. I'll go to the V.P.'s office. Anything's better than listening to your boring voice."

"Go. If I find out that you didn't go, you'll get ten days suspension added on to whatever punishment they give you."

Bone walked toward the vice principal's offce, then right past it, and out to the parking lot where he stole the first bike he came to that wasn't locked. He yanked it out of the rack, then climbed on and started pedalling. He drove the bike onto Old Wilson Highway and then started heading toward Thirteen Bends Road and his retreat, the room.

Tony and Pam made it to their car ahead of the people attending the strange services. But when Tony looked back toward the woods he saw a couple of the hooded people pointing at them and walking quickly toward the car.

"Let's go," Tony said, not wanting to be identified. Pam started the engine and threw the gear shift into drive. The small car lurched forward and the wheels caught the pavement. The tires squealed and the Metro sped down the road. Tony looked back expecting the members to follow them in their cars, but they just stood in the middle of the road. Silent black figures. He was glad that Pam had suggested taking her car. If they had taken the van, someone would have surely recognized it.

"What was that all about? Why did they start after us?" Pam asked.

Tony shook his head. "They probably thought we were messing around with their cars or something."

"What if they saw us leaving the ceremony and didn't want us to tell anyone about it?"

"Now why would they do that?"

"I don't know. Maybe, well . . . I don't mean to be disrespectful, but those services were . . . well, pretty strange. Do you think . . ."

"Do I think what?"

"Never mind."

"I know," Tony ran his thumb across his bottom lip. "Do I think that Aunt Ann was in some kind of a cult or something?"

"It was kind of, well, strange don't you think and sort of scary?"

Tony shook his head. "It's just so messed up. I can't imagine my aunt into something like that. I mean she was always talking about God. Shoot, anytime one of the televangelist guys was on TV, she would get mad and say how phony religion was becoming and stuff like that."

"But the way they were talking in that weird language," Pam said. "It sounded like a religious ceremony of some kind."

"I can't believe my aunt was in a cult. Maybe it wasn't a religious group. Maybe it was one of those clubs, like the Society for Anachronism. You know like Mr. Bates the history teacher talks about where people pretend to be part of medieval times. They have sword fights and tournaments."

"That could be, I guess," Pam said, although she suspected that Tony's aunt didn't want him to attend the services because she *was* a member of a cult.

"Aunt Ann never mentioned it, but she was always going out and stuff before she got sick. She could've been part of it. She did have a lot of old junk in the attic."

"Why don't we go look at the stuff in the attic and see if we might be able to figure something out from

166

that."

"We can't. The lawyer guy says they took that stuff away yesterday. Aunt Ann was giving it to charity."

"Oh."

Tony shook his head and sniffed a laugh. "I wanted to say goodbye to my aunt, and I find out that I needed to say hello."

"What do you mean?"

"I mean it seems like I didn't even know her. She's into this thing and I didn't have a clue."

"Even if your aunt was into a religious sect or something, that doesn't mean it was a bad thing," Pam said as she turned off Cross Road onto Old Wilson Highway. "It could've been just something different from the mainstream. She probably didn't tell you about it because she wanted you to make your own decisions about religion." She didn't believe it, but hoped Tony might.

Tony nodded. "Maybe."

As they approached the entrance to Cooper High, Pam pointed ahead of them.

"Hey, isn't that Bone?" she asked. He was on a bike, heading down Old Wilson Highway toward Thirteen Bends Road.

"Yeah. It is."

"But didn't you guys drive to school together."

"Yeah, we did and that's not his bike. Pull up beside him."

Pam caught up with Bone and Tony rolled down his window. "Bone! What's up, man? Whose bike?"

"I borrowed it," he said coldly. The tone of his voice was spooky.

167

"Where are you going?" Tony asked.

Bone turned and looked at his friend. "To the room at the club."

"The Night Owl Club? You mean you're skipping?"

"So?" Bone said irritably. "What are you two doing?"

Tony looked at Pam, then back at his friend. "Nobody goes to the club during the day. There won't be anybody there."

"Yeah, there will be."

"You mean your girl and her friends? How do you know?"

"I just do. Now leave me alone."

"But, Bone . . ."

Bone slammed on the brakes of the bicycle sending up a fishtail of dirt and leaves. He turned and stared at the two kids in the car. "School sucks. I don't need it! I'm blowing it off! Now I'm going so I'll see you later. You guys don't know. You just don't know."

Bone started to pedal away from the car.

"What don't we know?" Pam asked Tony.

Tony shrugged. "Man, on top of my aunt dying and all this stuff I'm finding out about her, Bone's flipping out. I never would have thought it, but he might be on something."

"Drugs? Bone would never do that."

"That's what I used to think, but it would explain a lot of his weird behavior."

"I just don't believe it."

"Yeah, well, he started acting funny after he met those girls. They might have turned him onto something," Tony said. "I can just see it. A couple of cute

168

girls take an interest in him and they pull out some stuff. Bone might have done some just to go along. I mean he's never had a girlfriend. One French kiss and he's somebody's slave. I know him. It would explain why he always wants to go to the club. Maybe he's getting hooked on something and they're supplying it."

Tony looked out the window and saw the vanishing figure of his friend. "Bone, you dipwad," Tony said. "I don't feel like dealing with this."

"Tony, maybe he's just skipping out one day to see his new girlfriend. It's not that big of a deal," Pam said, realizing that Tony was at the end of his emotional rope. "You've been under a lot of stress lately."

"I know and it wouldn't be that big a thing if he wasn't acting so different. Let's go park in the school lot for a little while and then we'll go to this room at the club that he's always talking about."

"Are you sure?"

"Yeah," Tony said, "Bone's my best friend and I don't want to lose him. I've had enough losses to last a lifetime."

Bone was slightly winded when he got to the Night Owl Club. He shoved the bike he had stolen into some bushes and caught his breath. The air was cool and hurt his throat as he breathed. Once he got his wind, he went into the club. The main room was deserted. Jake Demos was behind the bar wiping glasses. For some reason, Bone felt compelled to hide from Demos. He hurried across the floor hoping that he wouldn't see him. He made it to the entrance to the back room and ducked inside the storage area.

Jake Demos turned and looked toward the room. He shook his head.

Bone ran across the ancient storeroom floor and opened the incongruous new door that led to the staircase. He stepped inside and closed the door behind him.

As Bone went down the stairs, he could hear music playing and smiled. He got to the platform and went to the door. He opened it and stepped inside. The sweet smelling mist enveloped him in a caress. He breathed deeply and looked around the room. All his friends were there, just like he knew they would be. He waved and everyone began smiling. The sea of grinning faces moved closer and swallowed Bone in a wave of love and admiration. Bone bathed in the sweet waters of acceptance.

Outside the club, Tony and Pam pulled into the parking lot and parked the Metro.

"Look," Tony said, pointing to a bicycle tire sticking out from the bushes.

"He's here." Pam replied.

"I never doubted it," Tony said grimly. He had a bad feeling about the whole situation. If Bone was on drugs he would more than likely be unreasonable. It would be difficult to get him to go with them and seek help.

The two teenagers went into the club. Jake Demos saw them come in and motioned them to come over to the snack bar.

"I didn't know school was out today," Jake said in a gruff tone.

"It's not."

"I know," he said, his eyes narrowing into slits. "You know we don't like kids skipping and coming into the club. It gets parents mad at us."

"We had to come. A friend of ours is here. We need to talk to him."

Jake nodded. "I saw him."

"Do you know where he is? It's some kind of room downstairs."

"You'll find it through that door. Your friend is there."

"Thanks," Tony said, then turned to Pam, "I want you to stay out here. It would be better if I talk to Bone one on one."

"Okay, but if he gets weirded out or something, come out here and get me and Mr. Demos or somebody."

Tony nodded and kissed her.

As Tony went through the door to the storage area, Demos watched him and smiled slightly. He wondered if he had the strength to deal with his friend's situation. Only time would tell.

Tony walked through the ominously quiet room until he saw the freshly installed door.

"That must be it," Tony said to himself as he went over to the door and opened it.

The stairwell was dimly lit. The light from the bare bulb by the door died before it made it halfway down the stairs. Tony looked back at the storeroom and then down the stairwell. He licked his lips and started down the stairs.

There was a certain amount of tension as he went

171

down the stairs. Tony didn't know whether it was from the eerily lit stairwell or the fact that he might be finding something about his best friend that he might not want to know. He came to the midpoint in the stairs. He could hear music coming from behind the door.

He took a step forward into a cold draft of air. A sickly sweet smell like rotting meat, was coming from the direction of the room.

It's probably a dead rat or something. That dead mouse that got caught in the air ducts at home smelled just like this.

Another gust of icy wind blew past his feet. It carried the smell of death.

Spooked, Tony started to go back up the stairs, but he stopped dead in his tracks when he heard Bone's laugh break through the eerie music.

"So you are in there," Tony whispered as he turned back toward the door and then slowly walked over to it. He grabbed the knob which was icy cold to the touch. He turned it and opened the door. Tony stepped inside the room.

Tony couldn't believe his senses. He was stunned. Too stunned to do anything but stare at the sights before him. The room was a nightmare. Cobwebs hung from every corner. The air was frigid and the rotten smell was overpowering. A bizarre screaming sound, like music, played from speakers long since eaten away by parasites. The throbbing beat underneath the screeching melody sounded like a huge heart.

Terrified, Tony saw his friend, Bone, out on the

172

dance floor. His dance partner was obviously a female judging by her tattered dress, but that was the only thing about her that even vaguely resembled a girl. Her face was nothing more than dried prune-like skin wrapped around a grinning skull. Her eyes looked like opaque sacks of glue. The hair on her head was matted and looked like it was made of stringy clay. The scrawny fingers of her skeletal hands clutched the back of Bone's head. The smile on Fenimore's face was the picture of contentment.

Tony started to scream at his friend to get out of there, but a skeletal hand clamped over his mouth. Eyes wide with fright, the scared teen turned and was face to face with the corpse of a teenaged boy.

Hey, Tony," the corpse said, in a raspy ethereal voice.

Tony couldn't speak. His vocal cords were taut with fear.

"I'm Jackie. Jackie Pressman." The creature extended a hand of lank and bone.

Tony backed away from the corpse that called itself Jackie while he searched the filthy floor for a weapon.

"You shouldn't have come here. The room's not for you," the thing in the Cooper High letter jacket rasped. "It's not for you at all."

Tony turned and screamed, "Bone! Bone! Help me, man!"

Bone stopped dancing with his macabre partner and looked toward his friend.

"That's my pal, Tony," Bone said to Ashley. He was blissfully unaware of the danger his friend was in.

"Tell him to go away," Ashley said.

"Why? He's been wanting to meet you. Tone, come here. I want you to meet Ashley."

"I wouldn't do that," Jackie said, in that unearthly voice. "Bone's one of us. He doesn't need you anymore."

"Shut up!" Tony said, grabbing an old stool and tossing it at the decaying body.

The stool hit Jackie square in the chest. He was rocked back as the stool hit the ground and broke into pieces.

Tony ran across the room and grabbed Bone.

"What are you doing?" Bone said, surprised by his friend's behavior.

"Can't you see them?" Tony shouted. "We have to get out of here!"

"Go? I'm not going anywhere."

"Bone, they're dead. All of them are dead."

Ashley reached over and grabbed Tony by the shirt. She pulled him toward her and gave him a mealy kiss. He could feel little things squirming against his lips. "That's a goodbye kiss," she croaked and then laughed until she lost several teeth.

Tony gagged and almost vomited. He backed away from the decomposed girl and walked straight into another one of the zombies.

"Tony, man, be cool, this is Ashley," Bone said, unaware that the girl had just lost an ear to rot. "And that's Lori." He pointed to the girl behind his friend.

"Bone!" Tony shouted as he slapped his friend's face as hard as he could in hopes that the pain would jar him into action.

174

It did.

Bone shouted with rage and threw a hard punch that caught Tony in the side of the head. He staggered and tripped on the remains of the rotten stool. Trying to break his fall, Tony slapped the floor like he had learned in judo class.

Before Bone could follow up, Tony jumped up and shouted at his friend again.

"Bone, this is all wrong, man! We have to get out of here!"

Bone shook his head and looked around him. Ashley seemed to quiver in the light. Her makeup drooped and he saw a glimpse of what lay underneath. Then her face shifted back to the pretty girl he knew.

"Nooooo!" he shouted as he charged Tony.

The enraged teen slammed into the bigger boy driving his back into one of the old tables. Pain shot up Tony's spine and for a brief frightening moment, he thought Bone had broken his back. But he could move and move he did. He spun around and shook Bone loose then shoved him back into a stack of chairs. They crumpled and shattered under his weight.

"Bone! I'm here to help you!" Tony shouted as Ashley charged him from behind. He easily evaded her clumsy attempt only to find that it was a ruse to get him to move to his left. Waiting for him there was another of the dead things. Only this one wasn't as decayed as the others. He still had some muscle and grabbed Tony in a waistlock. Tony lifted his legs to shift his weight and loosen the thing's grip, another

175

move from judo class. The thing was unable to hold him. Tony slid out of its grasp and grabbed Bone by the arm.

"Let's go!" he shouted.

Bone looked at him, his eyes wide and confused. The room shifted and wavered like a heat mirage on the highway. He saw cracks in the wall. Dust covered the table tops. He saw Jackie's letterman jacket and the grinning corpse wearing it.

"Now, Bone!"

"Don't go, we need you," Ashley said to Bone in that sweet voice that sounded to Tony like fingernails on a blackboard. "We love you."

The room reeled. The sweet smell of the mist filled Bone's nostrils. The beautifully faceted glass globe twinkled hypnotically.

"Bone, don't . . ." Tony said, seeing his friend's expression change from confusion to contentment.

"We love you. You're the best."

"Please," Tony pleaded.

Bone's face contorted with rage. He lashed out and caught Tony in the stomach with a punch. A web of pain spread through Tony from the center point of the blow. Bone growled and threw another punch at his best friend.

Falling backward, the stunned teenager dodged the second blow and managed to grab Bone's belt. Tony yanked hard and pulled Bone toward him. Shifting his weight, he slammed Bone into the wall. The teenager's head hit the concrete, knocking him out cold. Tony grabbed the limp body and tried to pick him up in a fireman's carry.

176

"Let him go, Tony!" a voice said, from behind him. Tony turned and the thing called Jackie grinned at him. In his hand was a sharp knife.

Tony let go of Bone setting him down gently. The other dead things moved in on them.

A scream erupted from the direction of the entrance to the room. The corpses stopped and looked at the shocked girl standing in the doorway. It was Pam. She had grown concerned and come down to see what was happening, but was totally unprepared for the appalling sights that greeted her at the door.

Tony seized the opportunity created by her sudden appearance. He stood up and reached out for the corpse of Lori. He hurled her into the knife wielding creature who tried to evade her, but was too slow. The two creatures fell in a tangle of withered flesh and bone. Tony grabbed Bone's arm and took off running for the door, dragging his friend behind him.

"Bone! Don't go! We love you!" Ashley cried.

"Get out, Pam!" Tony shouted at his paralyzed girlfriend. Her eyes were riveted on the crumbling teenager crawling toward her.

"Pam! Go to the car!"

Pam heard Tony's voice and abruptly snapped to attention. She saw the corpse approaching her, spun on her heel, and took off running for the stairs.

"Go to the car and start it!" Tony shouted, hoping that she heard him. "Wait for us."

The corpse stopped and turned to face Tony. The teenager let go of his friend and lashed out with a kick that snapped the zombie's leg. It crumpled and fell to the floor. Tony grabbed Bone's arm and

177

dragged him through the doorway. He slammed the door shut. The corpses were screaming in the room, and Tony wondered how long they would remain there. He bent down and picked Bone up, hoisting him over his shoulder. Staggering under the load, Tony made slow progress up the stairs, but eventually made it to the top. Shifting Bone's weight to allow him to open the door, Tony opened it and went into the storeroom. He felt like putting Bone down, but the thought that the creatures might be coming spurred him onward. He ran into the main room of the club and then out into the parking lot.

From a darkened corner in the main room, Jake Demos watched with interest, but did nothing to interfere.

Pam saw Tony and Bone come out of the club and drove over to pick them up. Putting on the emergency brake, Pam got out and opened the back door. Tony put the groggy Bone into the back seat. The stunned teen was beginning to regain consciousness. Pam got into the driver's seat and Tony jumped into the passenger seat of the car. Pam released the brake, put the car in gear, and roared out of the parking lot. She drove down Thirteen Bends Road trying to keep from going too fast on the treacherous hairpin turns.

"What were they?" Pam asked her voice taut with fear. "What were those things?"

"I—I don't know," Tony stammered. He tried to make sense of what they had seen, "Dead things. Kids. They were, like, corpses of kids."

"But they were alive," Pam said, trembling.

"I know, but how? And why didn't Bone see them

178

the way we did?"

"Tony, let's go to the police and tell them."

"That we saw a bunch of dead kids attack us? They'd never believe us."

"But we saw them."

"I know, but somehow I know if we brought the police they wouldn't be there or they'd be normal like Bone sees them."

"Why didn't we see them as normal then?"

"I don't know. Maybe . . ." Tony struggled to come up with an answer, but failed. "I just don't know. Maybe, they weren't expecting us."

Suddenly, the tires slipped off the pavement and rumbled on the shoulder. Pam steered them back onto the road.

"Are you okay to drive?" Tony asked.

"I'm shaking, but I can do it."

"Bone's house is pretty close. Let's go there and try to figure out what's going on."

As they arrived at the Fenimores' house, Bone began to stir in the back seat.

"Whuh happen?" the teenager mumbled from the back seat. He sat up rubbing the top of his head. He felt a large lump. "My head."

"You okay, Bone?" Tony asked.

"My head is splitting. Wh—what's going on?"

"You don't remember?"

"Yeah, I was in the room and you came in . . . and . . . and you started a fight with my friends."

"You didn't see anything . . . strange?"

Bone started to get mad. "Yeah, I saw my best friend push a girl into my friend, Bob. And I saw you

179

hit Jackie Pressman with a chair."

"Bone, you didn't see those *things?*" Pam asked.

"What things? What are you guys talking about?" Bone said. "Why'd you come in and start trouble, Tone?"

"We have to talk. There's something about that room. Something awful. Let's go in the house."

Bone sighed and started to get out of the car. The trio walked up to the front door. Bone unlocked it, and they went into the house. In the living room, Tony and Pam sat on the couch. Bone sat in the chair opposite it.

"So what is this crap about the room?" Bone said, angrily.

"That room. There's something about it . . ."

"Yeah, so you said," Bone sniffed. "Man, you really are jealous. I mean we're still friends and everything, so why the attitude?"

"Bone, the kids in that room! They're dead!" Tony shouted.

"What?!" Bone shouted.

"I know it sounds crazy, but when I went into that room I saw corpses of kids walking around. And you were . . . you were dancing with one of them."

"Man, that is crazy," Bone said.

Tony shook his head. "I don't know what's going on, but you can't go back there."

"I swear I saw them, too," Pam said. "It was awful."

"I've been there a lot of times. They're just high school kids," Bone said, although his confidence was beginning to waver as he recalled incidents where he

180

thought he was seeing things in the room. Rotten things.

"Then how come you don't have any of their phone numbers?"

"Just don't," Bone said as Tony added to his confusion.

"Have you ever seen your new 'friends' at school?" Tony asked.

"Look, man, do you think I would keep going to a room full of dead kids?" Bone said, trying to come up with reasons to deny his friend's allegations. "You're just starting trouble. Playing some sick joke that I wouldn't even do."

"No, we're not. You're my pal, man, I wouldn't joke about dead people, especially not right after my aunt just died."

Pam added, "I swear we saw them. It was for real. I don't know why or how, but those things were alive. Ghosts or something."

"Bone, you can't go back there to that room," Tony said sternly.

"I don't believe any of that crap. You both must be seeing things or something."

"We didn't see things. It was real. The girl she . . . she kissed me," Tony recoiled as he recalled the disgusting feeling of the girl's kiss.

Bone was confused. On one hand, he knew that the people in the room were his friends and that they adored him, but on the other hand, he had seen some strange and frightening images in the room from time to time.

"So what if I believe you that something's weird

about the room. What do we do about it?" Bone asked.

"I don't know. I just don't know. But I do know one thing."

"What's that?" Bone said.

"You can never go back to that room again."

Just then, the doorbell rang causing the trio to jump. They looked at each other. No one moved to answer it.

The bell rang again.

"What should we do?" Tony said as visions of zombies filled his head.

Whoever was at the door knocked on it.

"Tony?" Pam said, looking into the frightened teenager's eyes.

"Tony, it's me. Mr. Goodfellow. Please answer the door," a voice said from behind the front door.

"It's that lawyer guy," Tony said as he got up from the couch and went to answer the door.

Tony looked at the peephole and saw the portly attorney. He opened the door.

"Hello, Tony."

"Hi, Mr. Goodfellow."

"Oh, call me Mr. Gee. After all, we will be seeing a lot of each other."

"Sure."

"May I come in?"

"Yeah, sorry, come on in."

Tony opened the door all the way and the fat man waddled into the house. He went into the living room and said to Pam and Bone, "How do you do? I'm Mr. Goodfellow."

"Hi," Pam said.

Bone waved.

"Tony, I need to speak to you about some things pertaining to your estate," the corpulant attorney said as he glanced at the two teens in the living room.

"We'll go up to my room," Bone replied, as he got up from his chair.

"That would be best," Goodfellow said.

"But I don't mind if they stay down here," Tony said, wanting the trio to stay together so he could keep an eye on Bone.

"It would be best that this remain confidential," Goodfellow said with a smile, then focused his attention on Bone. "You understand, don't you?"

"Sure," Bone said.

"But we need to hang together, he might . . ." Tony replied.

"He might what?"

"Tony, I won't go back there today," Bone said, seeing that his friend was starting to freak.

"You swear?"

"Yeah," Bone said. "Swear to God."

"Cool." Tony replied. Then he unexpectedly hugged his friend. Bone grinned abashed by the show of affection. Goodfellow smiled, but it didn't touch his eyes.

Bone started up the stairs as Pam went over to Tony and whispered in his ear, "I'll keep an eye on him."

She kissed Tony's cheek and then joined Bone upstairs.

Tony noticed that the front door was slightly ajar. "Just a sec," he said. "Let me get the door. It sticks

183

sometimes."

Tony got up and went to the door. When he opened it to slam it shut, he noticed the black Porsche parked in his driveway. The car seemed familiar to Tony, but he couldn't put his finger on where he had seen it. His mind was still a jumble of contradictions and suppositions about the day's events. He slammed the door and went back into the living room where he found Mr. Goodfellow sitting on the couch. The cherubic little man smiled and motioned for Tony to sit down on the couch beside him.

"How are you doing?" Goodfellow inquired.

"Pretty good," Tony lied.

"That's good. Good."

"So what's up?" Tony said.

"Just need you to sign some papers and things. Then we need to go over your procedures in case you need emergency funds. Just trifling details really."

Tony liked the fat man and thought about telling him what he had seen at the room. He seemed to recall seeing something about attorney/client privilege on one of those law shows on the tube. If he told him, it would remain confidential. He decided to test the waters. "Mr. Goodfel—uh, Mr. Gee, do you believe in ghosts?"

Goodfellow raised an eyebrow. "Ghosts?"

"Yeah, spirits and stuff like that."

"Why no. What makes you ask?" The fat man smiled curiously.

Tony could tell by the expression on the attorney's face that he didn't believe in such things. He decided to keep his mouth shut about what he had seen. "Oh,

184

nothing, we were just talking about it at school to-day."

"I see. Well, that's all very interesting, but we have to get down to brass tacks."

Goodfellow started going over the matters that he had come to discuss with the young man. Tony tried to concentrate on what the attorney was saying, but couldn't get the room out of his mind.

"Now about the title to your van, Tony."

"Huh?" Tony said, snapping to attention.

"Your van. We need to change the title so . . ."

"Oh, man, the van," Tony said, interrupting Mr. Gee as he suddenly recalled that he had left the van parked in the school's lot.

"What's the matter?" Goodfellow said.

"I left the van at school. Me and Pam, uh, we kinda skipped."

Goodfellow nodded. "At times like this, school does seem unimportant."

You're not kidding, Tony thought.

Goodfellow continued. "I tell you what. I'm going by the school on my way home, I could take you to get your van.

"Oh, that's okay, uh, I can get it later." Tony didn't want to leave Bone.

"It's no problem. We're pretty much done here. And I need to check the van's mileage. Let's go." Goodfellow struggled to his feet and gathered up his papers.

"Oh, no, really, I don't want you to go out of your way for me," Tony said.

"I insist. Now come on."

Tony considered the proposition. I do need to get the van, but I don't want to leave Pam and Bo . . . Wait a minute, I'm not thinking straight. They can come with us. "Okay, let me go get Bone and Pam and we'll go."

Mr. Gee frowned, "Oh, I'm sorry. I didn't tell you. My car's a two seater. I don't have room for four."

Tony didn't really want to leave Pam and Bone, but he did need to get the van, and it was a short drive. He would be back in less than half an hour. Surely Bone would be all right for that long.

"Let me go tell them what's up and I'll be ready to go."

Mr. Gee smiled as he watched Tony run up the stairs.

Tony went into the bedroom where Bone and Pam were sitting on the bed.

"Hey, is that guy gone?" Pam said, when she saw her boyfriend.

"Not yet. Listen, he offered to give me a ride to school to get the van. I should be back in a half hour."

"You want us to go?" Pam asked.

"Yeah, but he's only got a two seater."

"I could take you."

"I know, but he's going that way and like I said, it's a short drive."

"I'll be cool if that's what you guys are thinking," Bone said. "I mean just because a guy hangs with ghosts doesn't mean he's whacky."

Tony and Pam laughed at the joke despite the terrible truth behind it. This sounded like the old Bone. Making jokes in the face of adversity. Maybe things

186

would be okay, after all.

"Okay," Pam said. "See you in a bit."

Tony kissed her.

"How about me?" Bone said.

"See ya," Tony smiled.

He left the room and went back downstairs where Mr. Gee was waiting for him. They got into the sports car and headed for Cooper High.

As the Porsche approached eighty miles per hour down Old Wilson Highway, Goodfellow looked over at Tony to see how he was reacting.

"Speeding is my one indulgence," he said.

Tony smiled and watched the speedometer creep past eighty-five.

"Don't worry. I'm an excellent driver."

"I'm not worried," Tony said, enjoying the ride. The rush from the car's speed made him temporarily forget about the day's incidents.

Goodfellow downshifted. The car whirred and slowed slightly. He pushed down the gas pedal and the car accelerated powerfully. He shifted quickly and the car responded with another burst of speed. "I love that feeling of power."

"It's pretty cool," Tony agreed.

"Would you like to drive the car?" he asked, smiling.

"This 944?"

"Certainly."

"Yeah," Tony said.

"Fine," Goodfellow said, as he slowed the car and pulled to the shoulder. He struggled out of the driver's seat and walked around to the other side of the sports car. Tony jumped over the gear shift and sat in the driver's seat. He revved the engine and heard the power.

"Are you sure?" the teenager asked, glancing hesitantly at the attorney.

"Enjoy," Goodfellow said, with a wave of his hand.

Tony put the car into gear and popped the clutch. The wheels squealed as they hit the asphalt. "Sorry," he said, smiling sheepishly. He hadn't meant to burn rubber, but the car had more power than he was used to controlling.

"Just enjoy," the portly attorney repeated as he leaned back in the seat.

Tony drove the rest of the way to school and saw his van parked in the lot. He roared into the parking lot, pulled up beside the van, and parked.

"Man, that was awesome. Thanks, Mr. Gee."

"I'm glad you enjoyed it."

"Well, I better get going," Tony said, grabbing the door handle.

Goodfellow reached over and took his arm. He smiled kindly. "There's just one more thing, a trifling matter really."

"What is it?" Tony said.

The smile dropped off of the jolly man's face. He leaned forward and whispered in a cold voice. "Leave Bone Fenimore alone."

Tony's guts knotted. His mouth dried up like he was chewing on a chalk sponge.

"Wh—what?"

"You heard me. Leave him alone."

"But . . ."

Goodfellow's features darkened. "Listen to me, Tony. I know you went to the ceremony this morning."

Tony suddenly recalled where he had seen the Porsche. It was parked on the side of the Cross Road woods. Goodfellow must have been one of the hooded people.

"I could hold up your trust until you're thirty. But I won't if you leave your friend alone. If not. Well, you don't want to hear about all that." Goodfellow grinned like a wolf.

"But, that room at the club . . . those kids—Bone didn't see that . . ."

The lawyer interrupted. "Forget about that room. And your friend Bone's in no danger. In fact, your aunt was the one who picked him."

"What?"

"She knew he would be perfect," Goodfellow said. "It was her wish that he be the one. Now you wouldn't want to ruin one of your aunt's last wishes."

"Aunt Ann picked Bone? For what?"

"That's not your concern."

"But those kids . . ."

"You are to forget about that!" Goodfellow's voice boomed. "Do you understand?" The cherubic features contorted into a mask of rage.

Terrified by the outburst, Tony nodded.

"If I or any of my friends find you interfering again, you will not like what happens. I assure you of that." Goodfellow glared at him and then his face relaxed into the elfin smile. He opened the passenger door and got out of the car.

Tony sat in the driver's seat, too stunned to move.

The day had twisted into a nightmare from which there seemed no escape.

"Oh, Tony," Goodfellow said, opening the driver's side door.

Tony looked at him.

"I know where the girl lives."

Tony's fear started to shift into anger at the implied threat directed toward Pam.

"Now, if you would please." Mr. Goodfellow motioned for Tony to get out of the car.

Tony got out and watched the lawyer as he struggled into his car. Mr. Goodfellow sat and rolled down the window.

"You will leave Bone alone or you won't like what happens," Goodfellow said pleasantly.

Tony nodded.

"Goodbye, Tony," said the lawyer as he rolled up the window, started the car, and drove off.

"You fat little pig," Tony said, his voice trembling with anger and fear. His mind reeled. What had his aunt been a part of to get involved with this man? And what had she picked Bone to do? He focused all his anger on one man. Goodfellow. Without pausing to think, Tony reached into his pocket and pulled out his keys. He ran to the door, unlocked it, jumped into the van and waited till the Porsche was almost out of sight before he started to follow. He wanted to see if he could find out anything that might help his friend.

Bone and Pam were in his room when the television suddenly clicked on and a picture started to fade into view. He watched with a mixture of fear and anticipation as the room at the Night Owl Club slowly came into view. All of the kids were staring out at him. Their faces were a reflection of their disappointment.

Pam didn't seem to notice. She listened to the stereo while she glanced out the window, waiting for Tony to get back to the house.

"Bone, come back. We miss you," Ashley said in a crystal clear voice.

Bone stared at the screen. For a moment, he thought that this couldn't be happening, but then, just like the times before, the mist began to spread from the screen and envelop him in its sweet comfort. He saw Ashley reaching out for him. Lori was there. Bob and Jackie waved and laughed as if he had just told them one of his best jokes.

Bob spoke, "Bone, your friend's jealous just like you said. Jealous. He thinks you're his property. His boy. We're your *real* friends."

"Tony has Pam, you have me!" Ashley said. "Come back."

Bone sat on the bed transfixed by the images that he saw on the screen. He wanted to go back to the club and be with them, but something in the back of his head warned him to beware. How could they be there on the screen? a tiny voice whispered. How?

"Bone, we're waiting. We want to have fun. Come on and make us laugh. Dance with us. I need you." Ashley's voice had a mournful tone as if she was hurting because Bone wasn't there.

"I can't," Bone said, although the reason he said it soon disappeared from his mind as Ashley reached out from the screen and caressed his cheek.

"Come on, Bone, I love you. Everyone loves you here. We miss you."

The mist seemed to get heavier. It clouded his reason. All he could think about was the room and his friends and the fun. Nothing else mattered. Smiling, Bone stood up and started to leave.

Pam turned from the window and saw Bone walking toward the door.

"Where are you going?" Pam asked.

Bone turned and smiled at her. "To the kitchen to get a drink. Do you want something?"

"No, I'm fine," Pam said.

Bone glanced at the screen and saw Ashley blow him a kiss. "Be back in a minute," he said to Pam.

"Okay," Pam said, as she pulled back the curtain and looked for Tony's van.

Bone hurried downstairs. He had to get to the room at the club. His friends needed him. He hustled for the front door.

Tony saw the Porsche turn and then disappear into the gaping jaws of a heavy iron gate. The gate slowly closed behind the sports car. Tony pulled up to the curb of the house next door and parked his van. He had to find out what was happening. Tony ran to the fence and jumped up to get a hold. His fingers caught the edge of the fence and he was able to pull himself up and over. He landed and immediately feared that there might be dogs. He braced himself to jump back over the fence if he saw the slightest sign of a guard animal, he waited a few tense moments.

Nothing.

He took a few cautious steps toward the house and once again waited for the sound of a barking dog.

Again he heard nothing.

Satisfied that it was safe to proceed, Tony scurried across the lawn. The sun was just beginning to dip into the horizon and cast long shadows creating welcome hiding places. Tony kept in the shadows as he worked his way to the side of the house to find an open window or a door.

As he crept along the side of the house checking windows, he saw up ahead of him what looked like a maze of manicured hedge in back of a tiled patio. French doors led into the house from the patio. Tony started for them when one of the doors opened.

Tony's heart thumped when he saw Goodfellow come out of the house. The portly attorney was wearing a robe and carried a strange looking bag in one hand and an intricately carved lamp in the other. Goodfellow entered the maze and disappeared into the trimmed hedges. Tony waited and then he, too, entered the maze. He wanted to find out what Goodfellow was doing.

As he wandered through the arboreal labyrinth, Tony kept close to the hedges in case he came upon Goodfellow and had to hide quickly.

Weaving his way through the maze, he heard Goodfellow say something. His heart jumped and he ducked into the nearest hedge. He waited, a lump of fear lodged in his throat. Sweat formed on his forehead as he waited for the attorney to find him.

Goodfellow said something else that Tony couldn't make out.

A bead of sweat dripped into his left eye. He wiped away the drop with the back of his hand.

As Goodfellow's voice carried past him again, Tony realized that the attorney was speaking in that weird Latin-sounding language that he and Pam had heard at his aunt's services. Tony even recognized the lawyer's voice as being the one who had been leading the chants. His stomach flipflopped as he thought about his aunt and her involvement with the bizarre group. *Why, Aunt Ann? Why?*

Tony had to see what Goodfellow was doing. He crept out of the bushes both thankful and alarmed that the sun had almost disappeared. The cover of darkness was welcome and yet, its properties of concealment worked both ways. Something could be watching him from the shadows and he wouldn't know it until it was too late.

The teenager followed the sound of Goodfellow's voice until he came to a bend in the maze. He turned and saw the flicker of lamplight against the branches of the hedge. He stopped and ducked behind the bushes. He peered out and saw Goodfellow standing in the middle of a pentagram shaped alcove in the hedge. His pinky white flesh reflected the light. He was naked. Tony felt his flesh creep as Goodfellow spoke unknown words from an unknown language. Two words repeated over and over.

"*Astoth-Ra. Astoth-Ra.*"

At that moment, Tony wished he had never followed the attorney. The hairs on the back of his neck danced and his scalp tingled with fear.

"*Astoth-Ra. Astoth Ra.*"

Every instinct in Tony's body cried out for him to leave. Leave! Make like a ghost and vanish! Get outta here! his mind shouted as he watched the frightening little man intone those bizarre words.

But he had to stay and see what he could find that might help his friend, even though remaining there could prove a fatal mistake. He watched as Goodfellow's eyes rolled back into his head.

"Astoth-Ra. Astoth-Ra. Ya te ka," the fat man said, thrusting his hands at the ornate lamp.

The flame in the lamp burned low for a moment and then something started to happen. The flame began to burn brighter and brighter filling the pentagram with orange light. Tony had to shield his eyes as the intensity of the illumination grew and with it, his dread.

As the flame suddenly died down, Tony had to clamp his hand over his mouth to stifle a scream. He felt heat on his inner thighs and realized that he had wet his pants.

Standing there in front of the naked Goodfellow was a . . . a . . . Tony didn't know what it was. The thing stood on two legs like a human being, but that was where the comparison ended,. This creature had skin that looked like mud covered with slimy algae. Large scaly appendages that might have been wings protruded from its mucky back. Muscles rippled under the slick skin only to reveal themselves to be large wormlike parasites that traveled inside. The creature's face was indescribable. A bubbling mess of eyes and teeth and boils dripping pus. It opened one of its mouths and a voice that sounded like two mo-

195

lars grinding a squealing rat came sliding out of the dripping maw.

"Your time is short," the thing said in that hideous voice. "Speak or die."

"I have another for you," Goodfellow said. It was obvious he was trying to keep an even tone of voice and failing terribly. "A boy. He's the friend of one of your devotees' sons. I touched her with the disease then convinced her that she would live if she delivered a boy to me for sacrifice."

Tony's eyes filled with tears of pain and rage. It was so hard for him to believe that his aunt had selected Bone to be sacrificed to this horrible thing. How could she? And why did she pick Bone, his best friend? He now realized why his aunt had always believed that she would be saved from the cancer that ate away her body. The pact that she had made with Goodfellow was supposed to have given her a second chance and yet the attorney betrayed her as she had betrayed Tony and his best friend. He stared at the fat little man that had caused all this hurt and vowed that he would pay for his treachery.

"The boy will be at the room at the prescribed hour?" the thing said, as its eyes surveyed the world around it.

"When the moon is in the second quadrant of Antilles," answered Goodfellow.

"Very good. Remember, Mr. Gee," he hissed the name scornfully, "fail to deliver the boy and your fat lives are forfeit."

"Yes," Goodfellow whispered.

"And several lifetimes of sin can be hell," the thing

said and then exploded with laughter from each of its mouths — a clash of sounds that chilled Tony's blood.

"Until tonight," the creature said, as it began to fade into a shadow.

" Yes. *Astoth-Ra*. Until tonight."

The creature continued to fade into the shadowy night. Then Tony heard Goodfellow say something that sent his heart pounding.

"You should try to hold your water, boy," he said as he sniffed the air and disappeared.

Tony crouched down and saw the naked Goodfellow bend down and grab something out of the sack he had brought with him. He pulled out a large knife and stood.

"You shouldn't have followed me, Tony," he said, although he didn't look in Tony's direction.

Tony tensed as Goodfellow bent over and picked up his robe. He slipped it on as he studied the bushes to see if he could find Tony.

"You can't get away from me. I know this maze. You don't. Come out now and I'll make it quick, painless even. Make me find you and I will skin you alive."

Tony slid further back into the bushes. His head felt light. It was all too much — his aunt's treachery, Bone as a sacrifice for some monster, this fat man stalking him with a knife. His brain felt like it was swimming in a vortex. He hoped that when he stood he wouldn't faint.

Goodfellow sniffed the air. "Tony, I can smell you, so make no mistake I will find you. If you cooperate, I might even let you live like I did the boy Merritt.

197

Although you might say that living that way isn't really living at all." Goodfellow smiled confidently.

The arrogant grin of the attorney made Tony angry. He scraped the ground and filled his hand with dirt. He waited until Goodfellow was close.

The fat man walked around the edge of the pentagram slowly, checking every shadow until he found the one that concealed his prey.

Tony clutched the dirt in his hand. It felt heavy. He wondered if he would have the strength to throw it.

Goodfellow continued his search. The smile on his face was one of sadistic pleasure. He looked like a well-fed lion searching for a hyena to kill for sport.

Tony moved as his leg started to cramp from crouching for so long.

The fat man smiled as he heard the sound of leaves rustling. He turned and saw a glimpse of Tony's shirt. Clutching the knife in a fat paw, he took a step forward.

"Where are you going in such a hurry?" Bone's mom asked as her son almost knocked her down on his way out the door.

"Out," Bone said, brushing past her.

"Wait a sec," she said, grabbing his arm. "I'll be serving dinner in a little while."

"I'm not hungry," Bone replied.

"Where's Tony?"

"I don't know. Now let me go," he said angrily as he wrenched his arm free.

"Now you hold on, Harold Fenimore. You don't talk to me that way."

"I'm leaving."

"Hold on there," she said, grabbing his arm again.

Bone whirled and caught his mother in the side of the head with an elbow. Her legs crumpled and she almost fell. Bone grabbed her by the hair and slammed her head against the wall. She was so startled by the unprecedented attack that she could do little to stop it. The blow seemed to make her dizzy, and in another moment, she fainted.

As Bone let go of his mother's hair, her face dragged down the side of the wall. She crumpled into a heap and Bone simply stared at her. Then he saw the car keys clutched in her hand. He wrested the keys from her grip and in a trance-like state went outside to drive her car to the Nightmare Club.

"I seeeee you," Goodfellow said, in a playful voice as he approached Tony's hiding place. Slowly, he walked over concealing the knife behind his back as if it were a surprise.

Tony's hand ached from clutching the dirt. He prepared to strike.

"Come on out, Tony, come . . ."

Tony exploded out of the bushes, throwing the dirt as hard as he could into the fat man's face. The force of the throw lodged little chunks of dirt underneath Goodfellow's eyelids. He screamed in pain as he dropped the knife and clawed at his face. Tony thought about going for the knife, but then something happened to make him stop.

Goodfellow cried out in the strange tongue then plucked his eye from the socket. He held the staring orb in his hand and smiled. He put the eyeball in his mouth and swirled it around to clean it. Then he put it back into the socket. He repeated this with the other eye.

Tony almost laughed at the absurdity of the sight before him, but his terror was too overwhelming. He turned and ran from the man who had just sucked his eyeballs clean.

"You can't get away, Tony!" Goodfellow shouted. "I'll find you."

Tony ran as fast as he could down the row of hedges. He could barely see in front of him, relying on instinct to make his way in the darkness. He turned the corner and was shocked when he ran into a dead end. The branches stabbed at his face as he pushed his way through the hedge. He could hear Goodfellow laughing behind him.

Bleeding from the hedge, Tony made it out the other side only to be confronted with another dead end. He turned and ran as fast as he dared down the length of the maze and turned left at the intersection. He could hear the laughter of the fat man. It seemed to be all around him. His breath came in ragged bursts as he turned another corner.

Goodfellow was there! Wielding the knife, the fat man lunged at Tony. The teenager turned his body to evade the blow, but was too slow. The knife tore into the sleeve of his jacket barely missing his skin. He spun away ripping the knife through his clothing. He scrambled to gain his footing as Goodfellow charged again with the knife. Tony started to run away, but then quickly shifted direction and ran straight at the attorney. Surprised by the sudden move, Goodfellow was too slow to adjust. Tony jumped up and slammed both feet into the fat man's chest.

"Whhuufff," Goodfellow gasped as he flew back into the hedge. He slashed with the knife and cut Tony's leg. The wound hurt, but wasn't deep. Tony took off running as fast as he could. He turned at the first bend and then turned again.

Dead end!

He cursed and spun around on his heel. The frightened teenager took off running again. He went to the end of the aisle and turned down the path he hadn't chosen. He ran until he came to another intersection.

Which way? Which way? his mind screamed.

He chose the left.

Tony raced down the path only to come to another dead end. His heart sank. He turned around and saw Goodfellow at the other end of the path.

"End of the line, Tony," Goodfellow said.

Tony had to cut through the hedge again. He stepped into the hedge and discovered that this section was made of thorny vines. He pushed his way through as the thorns ripped gashes in his face and arms. The vines were thick and difficult to break. Tony feared he wouldn't be able to get through.

Goodfellow approached.

Tony fought with the branches forcing his way past as their thorns ripped his flesh. He could swear that the vines were alive. They seemed to anticipate his moves and block them. His skin was on fire as he continued to fight.

Enjoying the hunt, Goodfellow laughed at the

struggles of his doomed quarry.

The laughter spurred Tony's anger. He growled and felt a surge of adrenaline course through him. He began flailing at the thorny vines, breaking them into pieces. He roared with madness as he fought his way out to the other side.

He could hear Goodfellow emit an incredulous grunt and allowed himself a smile. The grin hurt as it stretched the cuts on his face. He could feel trails of blood sliding down his cheek and neck. He had to get out of the maze. He turned and was amazed to discover that he *was* out. He was free from the trap.

Spotting the fence, Tony took off running. He sprang to the top and grabbed it. As he pulled himself over, he looked back and saw Goodfellow emerge from the maze. The fat man's face was twisted with frustrated rage. Tony couldn't resist flagging him a one fingered salute before jumping to the other side of the fence.

Tony landed hard and rolled. He got up, brushed himself off and headed for the van. He got in and cranked the engine. It roared to life and screeched away. Tony had to get back to the Fenimore house before it was too late.

Pam heard a banging sound coming from downstairs. She heard the front door slam shut and looked out the window to see if someone was leaving. She saw Bone heading for his mom's car.

"Oh, no!" she gasped, knowing that Bone was going back to the club.

She threw open the window and shouted, "Bone,

don't! Don't go!"

Bone looked up at her and smiled as he got into the car, started it, and pulled out of the driveway. Pam turned and started to run out of the room. She bounded down the stairs and then stopped dead in her tracks when she saw Bone's mom lying on the floor of the foyer.

"Oh, no, Mrs. Fenimore!" She ran over to the fallen woman, hoping that she wasn't dead.

Enraged, Goodfellow watched the son of a disciple of *Astoth-Ra* insult him and then jump over the fence to temporary safety. Under ordinary circumstances, he would've pursued him, but tonight was anything but ordinary. It was the night he was to trade another teen's soul to *Astoth-Ra* in order to add another sixteen years to his life. The same number of years the teen had lived on earth. He would deal with Tony Sims later. Now he had to get to the room at the club and perform the ritual of rejuvenation. He ran into the house to get ready.

Tony's mind raced as fast as the engine of the van as it sped to the Fenimore residence. He had to get back to Bone's house and prevent his friend from going to the room at the club. Tonight was the night that the thing said the ritual was to take place. Tony didn't know exactly what it all meant, he just knew that Bone was to be sacrificed and that was enough to force him into action.

When Tony saw Pam holding a cold towel on Mrs. Fenimore's forehead, a sick feeling came over him.

203

"Tony, oh my God, Bone, he . . . he attacked his mom. I came down and she was just lying here . . . I can't get her to wake up."

"Oh no."

"I called 911 and somebody's on the way." She looked into Tony's eyes. "Tony . . . Bone . . . he went back to that place."

"Oh, man, we've got to get him out of there. Goodfellow's some kind of witch man or something."

"Goodfellow, that attorney?"

Tony nodded. "He's going to sacrifice Bone to some demon thing. It's so messed up." Tony quickly explained what had happened trying to make it sound believable in the face of its incredible implausibility. He told her about the appearance of the creature called *Astoth-Ra* and how they were going to somehow trade Bone for more life for Goodfellow. "My aunt was part of it. That's the most horrible thing. She was the one that told them about Bone. She thought she could use him to gain life, but they must've tricked her."

"I can't believe it," Pam said, stunned by the revelations.

Tony shook his head. "I have to go to that room and get Bone out of there somehow."

"We should call the police."

"And tell them what? That a prominant attorney's going to sacrifice Bone to some demon?"

"We don't have to say that. We can lie and tell them something else. Just so long as they go to the club."

"But Goodfellow will just make them see what he wants them to see."

204

"So why did he let us see those dead kids?"

"He wasn't expecting us. But he would be expecting the police."

They heard the sound of an approaching siren.

"So what do we do?"

"I'm going to the club."

"I'm going with you."

"No way. You have to stay here and help Mrs. Fenimore."

"The ambulance is coming. If I stay, I'll have to explain how she got hurt and they'll go after Bone."

"Pam, I can't let you. I don't want to lose you."

"But Tony . . ."

"Pam, I—I love you. I always have. Please don't ask me to let you go."

"Oh, Tony, I love you so much. I can't let you go alone. I can help. Two people have to be better than one. I might be able to distract them or something."

"Pam, this is a nightmare. Dead kids and some kind of demon. Chripes, the fat guy can pull his eyes out of his friggin' head. I don't know what chance we have even if I do take you with me."

The ambulance pulled into the driveway.

Pam said, "We have to try. Bone's our friend."

"Okay," Tony sighed. "But let's try to get something to fight with."

"My dad has a bow and arrow."

"Where is it?"

"In his bedroom closet."

"Let's go."

Tony left the door open so that the paramedics would see Mrs. Fenimore. Then he and Pam ran out

205

the back door.

At Pam's house, Pam went upstairs to get the bow, while Tony went into the kitchen and found a set of knives. He chose a butcher knife and a long thin filet knife. He tucked the butcher knife into his belt and carried the filet knife.

Carrying the bow, Pam came down the stairs. The compound bow was a formidable-looking weapon with a system of pulleys that made it easy to use. The razor-tipped arrows she carried looked deadly. Suddenly, Tony was struck by the notion that he and Pam might actually have to kill Goodfellow — to shoot him with the lethal arrows.

"Are you ready?" Tony asked, wondering at the same time whether he was.

Pam nodded.

"Let's go."

"Wait, we can't go into the club carrying all this stuff. Demos would never let us in there."

"You're right," Tony said. "Have you got any wrapping paper?"

"Wrapping paper?"

"Sure, we'll wrap this stuff like it's a gift. Say we're celebrating my birthday."

Pam smiled. "Good idea."

Nine

Tony and Pam were thankful that the Night Owl Club wasn't crowded. They carried their packages into the main room. Jake Demos watched them with a baleful eye then went back to pouring a soda. Jenny looked over at her father and caught his attention. She nodded. He shook his head and went back to his business.

Tony and Pam acted as though they were going to sit next door to the pool room, but they kept going and entered the storage room. Tony unwrapped the packages. He handed Pam the filet knife and tucked the butcher knife into his belt. Tony clutched the bow and then strung it. He tested the pull and found that the pulleys made it easy to get full power.

He strung an arrow and looked toward the door. "Okay, I guess we go."

Pam nodded again. She had lost her voice to the terror running rampant through her body like a virus. On quivering jelly legs, she followed Tony to the door.

Tony hesitated as he grasped the knob. He looked

back at Pam who stared at him with wide eyes. She clutched the knife and motioned for him to open the door. Tony licked his lips and opened the door.

As the two made their way down the creaking steps, Tony pulled the bow back and prepared to fire.

The closer they got to the midway point, the louder the screeching music became. The air chilled and swirled around their feet as they stepped onto the platform leading to the door to the room.

Pam hestitated, grabbing Tony's arm as he stepped forward.

"Tony, wait," she whispered.

"What?"

"I—I don't think I can do it. My whole body's shaking so bad I can hardly walk. Let's go back and get help."

The music screamed.

"It'll be too late," Tony said.

"How do you know?"

"I don't, but I can't risk it."

"Please . . ."

"I have to help Bone." Tony said as he grabbed the knob and pulled.

The door was locked!

He hadn't even considered that possibility.

"Locked," he said. "They must be getting ready to do it. Come on!"

"Where are we going?"

"To get the key."

Tony left the knives, and the bow and arrows hidden inside the storeroom as he and Pam went to find Jenny Demos. He knew she was nice and probably wouldn't ask questions.

"Jenny," Tony said when he found her wiping a table.

"Hey, what's up, guys?" she said.

"We need the key to the room downstairs."

"Downstairs?"

"The stairs leading from that storeroom back there," he said, pointing in the direction of the room.

"We don't have a key to that room."

Tony's heart sank. "But we have to get in there."

"I know," Jenny said cryptically.

"How . . . ?" Tony asked, startled by her revelation.

"Let it be, Jenny," a deep voice said.

Tony and Pam turned and saw Jake Demos standing there.

"But . . ." Jenny protested.

"Let it be," Demos commanded. "Remember the pact."

Jenny nodded as her father walked away to disappear into a shadowy corner.

"You have the key," she whispered. "Look for it close to your heart. That's where you'll find it."

"Wait," Tony said as Jenny walked away quickly. "Jenny, tell me what it is. Please, my friend's in danger."

Despite Tony's pleas, she didn't turn around to face him.

"What was that all about?" Pam asked, her voice trembling.

"I don't know, but we have to go back down there and try to figure it out."

"Tony, we should call the police."

"There's no time for that. They could kill Bone any minute," Tony said. He grabbed her hand and ran to the storeroom. Picking up the bow and handing the filet knife to Pam, Tony hurried over and opened the door. He was about halfway down the stairs when he saw a dark shape coming up. He drew back the bow and got ready to fire.

"Don't shoot," a voice called out from below them.

"Bone!" Tony shouted, recognizing the voice.

"But, Tony . . ." Pam said confused by Tony's shout.

"Tony, man, am I glad to see you," the voice said, as footsteps ran up the stairs.

"That's not . . ." Pam said as Tony interrupted her.

"Bone, I thought you might be dead."

"I am," the corpse of Bone Fenimore said, as it howled and then charged the two teens.

Pam screamed.

Tony drew back the bow and fired. The arrow hit the dead thing in the stomach and passed through its body. The corpse struck Tony full force knocking him back into Pam. She screamed and fell to the side. The thing reached past Tony and with a decayed hand of lank and bone and grabbed Pam's wrist. It tugged on her arm and sent her tumbling down the stairs into the darkness. Tony pulled the butcher knife out of his belt and drove it into the thing's neck. It howled.

But not with pain.

With laughter.

Tony's skin crawled as he pulled the knife and struck again with the same result. The giggling corpse grabbed him by the throat and pulled him close. Tony gagged when he saw the wormy-pocked face of his best friend. Bone smiled.

"Thanks for coming, Tone, I love you, man," the corpse said, laughing.

Suddenly, the words of Jenny Demos struck Tony with the force of a sledgehammer. *The key is close to your heart.*

Yes.

It has to be.

The creature's fingers tightened around Tony's neck. Trying to breathe, Tony tugged at his necklace. He found the charm at the end of it and ripped it from the chain.

The thing howled and squeezed.

As Tony thrust the funny bone charm that Bone had given him into its face, the corpse withered and backed away. The corpse's face began to crumble as Tony kept it at bay. A chunk of nose decayed and landed on the floor. Tony smiled and ground it underfoot. He drove the thing back.

"Pam, are you okay?" he called out into the darkness below him.

"She's dead," the corpse said, but the voice wasn't Bone's.

"You lie," Tony hissed.

"Broke her neck on the fall. Ain't that a shame,"

the thing giggled.

"Pam!"

"Dead and gone," the corpse laughed as Tony heard someone pounding on the door to the room. The corpse frowned.

"Help!" Bone cried from inside the room. "Somebody help me."

Tony thrust the charm at the cadaver, driving it back. He spun on his heel toward the door. He stuck the funny bone charm into the lock of the door, then turned it. The latch on the door unlocked. He grabbed the door and opened it. Bone almost tumbled out of the door, but was stopped by Bob and Jackie as they grabbed and held him.

"Tony! Help me!" Bone screamed as the two corpses dragged him back into the room.

Tony took a step toward his friend.

A fat fingered hand grabbed him.

He turned and saw Goodfellow standing there. He had somehow impersonated the corpse of Bone.

"Give me that," the fat man growled and reached for the charm.

Tony was too quick. He evaded the grasping paws of the lawyer and then abruptly jammed the charm into the fat man's eye.

The scream that Goodfellow uttered was one of sheer terror. It echoed through the long dark stairwell filling it with the sound of pain, panic, and defeat. Goodfellow spun around and fell against the wall. He whirled in a tight circle as he clawed at the charm in his eye, but couldn't remove it. He began to wail in that strange tongue, screeching words from a long dead language. Profane curses.

In the room, the zombie teenagers howled and released Bone. He tumbled to the ground and watched as Goodfellow screeched in a thousand voices of torment. Goodfellow began to erode like a sand sculpture in a windstorm. His skin desiccated and fell to the floor, followed by fatty tissue, then muscle, then bone all disintegrating into a rotten sulphuric powder, a stench from the bowels of hell. The gold charm clinked as it hit the steps.

Tony backed away as the strange cold wind swirled from the room and pushed the foul smelling dust against the wall. He turned from the rotting mess and then realized with horror that Pam was dead, another person he had cursed with his love.

Bone crawled to his side and put his arm around his miserable friend.

"Pam's dead," Tony said, as his voice cracked, "He—he threw her down the stairs."

"No," Bone said, feeling his eyes brim with tears. "Let's go look. She might just be hurt."

"No! I can't see her like that . . . I—I just can't."

"She might be hurt!"

Tony was inconsolable. "I knew I shouldn't have let her come. I knew it," he said as he began to sob.

"Tony, man, we have to find . . . oh my God!" Bone gasped as his face paled.

The sudden change of expression snapped Tony out of his grief. He whirled and saw the dust swirl up from the floor and start to form an obese body. The muscle and bone began to knit together crackling like a fire of tinder. The new layer of skin began to cover this sizzling flesh and bone like a spreading pink oil spill. Goodfellow's face began to form revealing a grin of both delight and deadly intent. His supposed death had all been a ruse to get the charm away from Tony.

As Goodfellow's vocal chords rejoined, he croaked in a bizarre half-formed voice, "Now where were we?"

Tony saw the glimmer of the charm. It teetered on the edge of the stairs. He tried to make a grab for it before Goodfellow regenerated completely.

But he was too late.

The corpulant warlock lashed out and kicked him in the side of the head.

A galaxy of stars exploded in Tony's skull as he tumbled down a few steps. The fat man moved with uncanny speed as he grabbed Tony by the arm and tossed him against the wall as if he were made of paper.

Laughing, he picked up the dazed Tony with his left hand again and pulled him close so that they were face to face.

"You've got a lot of guts, Tony," he said, holding his right hand up as the fingers changed into razor-sharp spikes. "Shall we take a look at them?"

Tony's eyes widened with terror as he stared at the dreadful spikes.

Goodfellow raised the hand and prepared to strike Tony dead when he felt a hot stab of pain against the side of his head. He screamed and slammed Tony into the wall, then dropped him on the stairs. He turned and saw Bone holding the charm. The spikes that were once his fingers turned inwards and dug into his palms.

"Get away from him," Bone said, his voice trembling.

"You're mine, Bone," Goodfellow said with Ashley's voice. "I love you. We all love you."

No. His mouth didn't move. It couldn't be . . .

Bone felt a hand on his shoulder. He turned. Ashley, pretty Ashley, was there.

"Bone, we're waiting for you," she said.

"You're not real. You're not."

"Oh, we're real, and you can stay with us forever. We can be together forever dancing and kissing, having fun. Forever."

A red cloud of sweet mist swept past Bone filling his lungs. He began to waver. The charm in his hand began to get hot. The pleasing mist swirled around him engulfing him in its spell. The charm felt like someone had lit a match to it.

"Give it to me," Ashley said softly. "Give me the charm."

The funny bone burned his palm. It hurt. Somewhere in the back of his mind, he knew that he shouldn't give it to her, but it was hot. Too hot to handle. His palm burned with fire.

"Please, Bone."

"No," Bone groaned as the charm started to sizzle his flesh.

"See how it burns. You're already a part of us. Give it to me."

Bone cried out from the pain. "No! I don't want to be!"

"You're already part of us."

"No. I don't want it," Bone screamed and slapped the charm into Ashley's hand.

She howled in agony as her fingers crumpled and burned. As her pretty features dissolved, she ran into the room taking the charm with her. Bone screamed as Goodfellow erupted into laughter. It was over.

He pushed Bone into the room.

"Tony!" Bone shouted to his friend, "Tony, help me."

Tony heard the scream and forced himself to his feet.

"Tony," a low voice said from below him. "Tony, help me."

It was Pam! She was alive!

"Tony! Help, oh God, help me!" Bone screamed as the corpses swarmed him and held him down and Goodfellow donned his black robe.

"Tony, my leg's broken," Pam cried.

"Hold on, Pam, I have to help Bone."

"Don't leave me!" Pam screamed afraid for her life.

"I—I . . ."

Just then, a bright light exploded from the room. It filled the stairwell with illumination. Tony saw Pam crumpled at the bottom of the stairs. Her leg was bent at a painful angle. He shielded his eyes as he looked into the midst of the light. He heard a strange whirling sound as the light seemed to be sucked back into the room. It moved with fierce speed and then disappeared into a black shadow.

"No," Tony said when he realized that it wasn't a shadow. It was a thing! A huge thing with mucky skin and what looked like a hundred mouths and eyes! It was *Astoth-Ra*.

"Where's the boy?" Ra said, in that unearthly voice.

"Just a moment and he'll be ready," Goodfellow said with the sacrificial knife in his hand.

"You had your moment," the demon said as Goodfellow prepared to strike.

"No, I will deliver him to you," the attorney shouted as he drove the knife through flesh and bone striking the beating organ that pumped life.

Tony looked away unable to bear the death of his friend. He heard a scream, but it wasn't Bone's voice.

"Noooooo!" Goodfellow screamed as he stared at the dagger sticking out of his chest. "No, I . . . I . . ." He stumbled and fell forward driving the dagger deeper into his fat body.

Tony ran into the room, shoving the stunned zombies away from his friend.

Astoth-Ra dug his claws into the obese man's blubber and picked him up. "I warned you, Mr. Goodfellow. Your time has come as I knew it would. Now I take back the lives that you expended for more time on earth and I give you a life of pain forever."

With those words, *Astoth-Ra* looked at Tony and Bone, smiled and then vanished in an explosion of light. Bone and Tony watched in silence as the corpses of the teenagers in the room crumpled into

217

dust and the room began to age in front of their eyes. After the transformation was complete, Tony turned to Bone and put his arm around him.

"Let's get out of here and go help Pam," he said, starting to walk toward the door. "I'm glad she's okay."

Bone nodded as he walked beside him. "Hey, Tony?" he asked.

"Yeah, Bone?"

"Do you think I might have a chance with Cindy if she knew I had dated an older woman?"

"Older woman?"

"Yeah, I guess Ashley had been dead for at least twenty years."

Shaking his head, Tony smiled. Bone was going to be all right, he thought as the two friends made it to the door and left the room . . . forever.

About the Author

Vincent Courtney wrote his first horror story, *The Glow on Mulberry Road,* when he was nine years old in the small town of Cocoa, Florida. After reading it, his parents knew that their son was destined for a career in horror or at the very least, a good job at the slaughterhouse.

An avid reader as a boy, Vince thrilled to the horror classics, Bram Stoker's *Dracula* and Mary Shelley's *Frankenstein* as well as the works of Edgar Allen Poe. In later years, Vince discovered the works of Stephen King, Peter Straub's *Ghost Story,* and Ray Bradbury's classic, *Something Wicked This Way Comes.* That last one gave him nightmares, even though he read it when he was thirty-two years old. Some of his other favorite books are F. Paul Wilson's *The Keep,* Richard Matheson's *I Am Legend,* and *The Vision* by Dean R. Koontz.

Vince now lives in Melbourne, Florida with his wife, Beth, and their pet vulture, Hortense. His adult novels include *Vampire Beat, Let's Pretend You're Dead, Wake Up Screaming,* and *Harvest of Blood.* In addition to being a writer, Vince is an accomplished television producer and director.

Vince likes to hear from readers. He, and everyone at *The Nightmare Club,* would enjoy knowing how you like the books, and what you'd like to see in future stories. Write to him, c/o The Nightmare Club, Zebra Books, 475 Park Avenue South, New York, NY, 10016. If you'd like a reply, please include a stamped, self-addressed envelope.

THE NIGHT OWL CLUB
IT'S COOL—
IT'S FUN—
IT'S TERRIFYING—
AND YOU CAN JOIN IT . . . IF YOU DARE!